This is a work of fiction. Names. ch~
incidents are either the pr~ '
or are used fictitiously. A
living or dead, events or

Copyright © 202

ISBN 9798395896797 (Paperback)
ISBN 9798395901781 (Hardback)

The Honourable Miss Penhall

Alexandra Kate

Dedicated to
All those who thought I wouldn't,
and all those that believed I could.

And

To Steven
whose endless belief fuels my life.

1
Natalie

The car cruised up the long driveway to the house. The road lined with aspen trees, drawing me ever closer to the sprawling mansion. I gazed at Brywood Manor, over 400 years old, the view instantly welcoming me home. Even though I had spent years away, it felt like no time had passed since I watched the grand house disappear in the rearview. The face of the house looked the same but there were small changes. The bright yellow flowers that had lined the lawns and framed the windows were gone. Replaced by dusty roses and sprays of white carnations. The lawns, as always, were immaculate but now two new statues sat in the front eaves of the gardens. My father, Lord Byron, on the left. And my mother, Lady Francis, on the right. I rolled my eyes as the car came to a stop; they would have been my mother's doing. I doubt my father even knew of their commission until they were situated in his front garden. That's how Lord Penhall liked things though. My mother could be stiflingly proud and very fussy at times, but as long as my father didn't have to hear any of it, he was happy.

The driver got out and I waited patiently for him to open my door. Pushing my chestnut brown hair back over my shoulder I stepped out onto the gravel path, I took a deep breath in, letting the fresh country air flood my lungs. Glad to be home.

Maria the head housekeeper was standing at the top of the stone steps. As I approached her she squeezed my shoulders, before looking me over.

"My Natalie, you are so beautiful, it feels like only yesterday I was saying goodbye to you." She had the beginning of tears in her eyes as she spoke, giving me a once over like she can't quite believe I'm here. Maria had worked and lived here as long as I could remember and, before I left, I had spent most of my time with her. My parents had always been busy when I was growing up so she had been the constant presence in my life. I felt tears growing in my own eyes.

"I've missed you." I greeted the ageing woman with a hug.

Pulling back, she shook the tears off. "How was your flight?"

"Long and thankfully over." I laughed lightly.

I had spent the last eight years working as an intern for a company based out of New York while I finished my business schooling at Cornell. I hadn't seen her in the years I had been gone. My parents had visited fairly regularly. We aren't exactly close but for one reason or another my mother would come over to America and she would drag my father along. She would spend the time out there for social calls or shopping. My father on the other hand, I don't know if she forced him to accompany her or if he genuinely wanted to see how I was progressing with my work. Looking at the house and Maria I was glad to finally

2

be home, but I couldn't deny that I would miss New York. It held a sense of freedom for me that I knew I wouldn't get now I'm home.

At 26 and seemingly home permanently, my duties would officially begin. Business school had been preparing me for the running of the estate and the various companies our family owned. And my mother had been preparing me for other duties. She had not once in all her visits neglected to tell me she was on the lookout for a husband for me. I had managed to stay her enthusiasm with the excuse of my being away. Now there would be no making peace with her. Arranged marriage was a tradition that our family still held to, so it wasn't a shock that my mother was anxiously waiting in the wings to secure me a profitable match. I had known about it my whole life, so you would think I would have grown used to the idea. I had not.

My time away had done more than solidify my opinion on this, I'd had boyfriends for a while but when it came to choosing a husband, I was expected to accept my mother's choice. I was nothing like my mother, and she nothing like me, so the prospect of this union made me nervous, to say the least. My only hope was she would pick someone for me and my personality, someone I could maybe grow to like. Love might be out of the question but at least someone I could relate to and bond with on some level. I wouldn't hold my breath. This was *my* mother here; she would pick whom she considered to be the best and hang what I thought of it.

I followed Maria into the foyer, a grand area with a double staircase leading to a beautiful oak-railed balcony. I had a reasonable apartment in NY, but it is not exactly a city known for spacious accommodation. It was difficult not to feel small when stepping into Brywood Manor, the grandeur of the place could be overwhelming but to me this was home. I let Maria lead me up the stairs, smelling the beeswax polish from the handrail and the soft scent of cookies drifting from the kitchen downstairs.

"Has someone been baking?" I inhaled the comforting aroma.

The housekeeper turned to me with a gleeful smile. "Yes, me." We had reached the top of the staircase and she turned to me. "I made some white chocolate cranberry cookies. I know they're your favourite...or they were before you left." She had a look of uncertainty in her eyes though it didn't creep down to her smile.

"Mmmm, they still are. You sure I must see my room now can't we just go and pig out on cookies?" I giggled and she joined in the laugh slightly smacking my arm.

"No, you have to see your new quarters. I can see I'm going to have to hide them just like when you were little." We both laughed at the memory and continued down the hallway. Pausing in front of a large set of double doors. This room was on the opposite side to my old bedroom. My mother had told me that I had been relocated and despite myself, I had a childish excitement to see my new room. Maria opened the doors with a flourish revealing a beautiful bedroom. The top of the walls had been painted a deep navy with white panelling lining the lower half. The bed matched this with white covers and navy throw pillows. A soft-looking white sofa sat in the centre of the room accompanied by 2 navy tall back armchairs. These faced a television hung over an ornate fireplace. Maria grasped my hand dragging me into the room. I continued to gaze around, it fit me perfectly not too girly and frilly but still feminine. Did my mother do this?

"It was mine and your mother's project," Maria spoke my thoughts from beside me. "She described your apartment back in New York and we went from there on what you might like."

"It's perfect, I'm shocked that Mother managed to refrain from pastel pinks and lace," I spoke running my hand over the back of the sofa.

"Well, I might have gently reigned her in at points. Floral lace was nearly on the cards with a great big pink canopy bed." I raised my eyebrows at the woman.

"You're joking?" I deadpanned.

Cracking a wry smile she laughed slightly "Yes, well about the bed the lace was a real struggle to compromise down to none!"

"Well, I for one am glad you did, this is perfect!"

"You haven't seen the best parts yet!" she waltzed towards the fireplace and 2 doors that sat either side "Left or right?" She glanced at me.

"Right first." She opened the door and stepped inside, I dutifully followed. Inside was a large dressing room and wardrobe. The theme of white and navy had carried through, though the navy was used more sparingly here. A huge island sat in the middle of the room surrounded by floor-to-ceiling cabinets. The island had pretty navy jars on it and drawers that I could see were already full of accessories and clothes. Some unopened gifts sat atop the marble island all wrapped in matching navy and tied with white ribbons. Maria didn't mention them, she didn't have to. Presents from my absentee parents. A sort of apology for not being here when I returned home, Maria though would have been the one to wrap them up. I barely acknowledged them; sure, I would open them later but after years of receiving presents in lieu of time I had begun to push them to the bottom of my to-do list.

"I've had your clothes that arrived last week put away already and will have someone put the rest away that arrived with you today," Maria spoke opening a few drawers to show me the contents. I wandered the room pulling open various drawers and cupboards. Filled with my old possessions and yet they somehow looked newer in the space. The whole room had been beautifully finished and dripped with luxury, despite liking to keep myself low-key I couldn't help but love it. Luxury and grandeur came with my heritage and birthright, but I never felt comfortable in it. Before leaving friends had gaggled on about the latest car they were driving or the newest bachelor on the scene who had *so much money* and I'm ashamed to say I would join in. Desperate to keep hold of friendships and the status that I had. My time in New York was the first time, excluding Maria, I had had truly organic adult conversation. It was refreshing and something I would dearly miss.

"Shall we?" Maria punctured my thoughts and gestured towards the door. Going back out into the main bedroom and then to the door on the left she opened this one with equal flourish. As I suspected it might be, it was a bathroom. It was equally large with a beautiful walk-in shower that could fit ten people and a bathtub that could give it a run for that money. The toilet sat opposite the sinks, yes plural, 2 to be precise. Ornate mirrors lined the wall above and soft towels, navy, were in a basket on the side.

"It is quite a bit bigger than your previous room," Maria spoke from the doorway.

"More than a bit bigger!" I commented on the expansive bathroom.

"I think your mother chose it with space in mind, seeing as she hopes you will be sharing it soon." Maria was now looking at me warily. I sighed eyeing the bathroom once again. The thought of sharing this with someone that I barely know isn't comforting. But it was inevitable.

"Hmm, I think I'll just have to enjoy having it to myself while I can then." I smiled reassuringly at her. Maria knew how much I worried over this arranged marriage, and I could tell that she also worried for me.

"I'll leave you to settle in, me and the cookies will be downstairs when you're ready." She smiled at me and excused herself. I decided to spend a little time familiarising myself with my new room. I unpacked my carry-on luggage, plugging in my phone charger and putting the few items I had packed in the small bag into their new homes. It wasn't much to do as most of my stuff had been sent ahead and the rest had yet to arrive, I was done quite quickly. With nothing left to do I practically skipped downstairs to find Maria and those delicious-smelling cookies.

2
Natalie

I sipped on my cup of tea, closing my eyes and enjoying the comfort. Yes, America had English Breakfast Tea, but Maria still made the best cup. I skewered some strawberries from my fruit salad popping them into my mouth, there was an early morning chill in the air, but it was not unpleasant. A light fog still hung over the expansive garden, and I could see, from my seat on the back patio, the morning dew sparkling on the lawn. I sighed fully content.

My eyes wandered over to the left of the grounds. The old stables, if you could call them that with all the renovations my mum had put into it, stood proud in the corner of the garden with white panelling and dark oak accents. Back paddocks I knew were there, were hidden by the tree line. The training pen was fully visible at the front of the building. I watched the sun cresting over the wooden building, movement by the entryway grabbed my attention. I turned my attention to the man walking into the stables, at the same time Maria came out to join me on the patio.

"Was that Mr Taylor I spotted just now?" I enquired over my shoulder.

"Mr Taylor?" She glanced in the direction of the stables where the man had already disappeared inside. "Yes, I imagine so at this hour." Mr Taylor had been the grounds manager here as long as I could remember and before him, his father had held the position. The post had been in his family for generations, with a son or nephew always taking the place. It was not something the current Lord had ever demanded of them; it had just always happened that way. The previous grounds manager training their heir to take over and then retiring when they were ready to. It was an arrangement that worked well for our family and theirs. I put my fork down and got up from my seat, meaning to head down to the stables myself.

"I'm going to go and say hello, it'll be nice to see him after all these years," I mentioned to Maria as I stepped onto the stone steps that led to the winding path. She absently nodded at me and continued to clear the breakfast things. She called to me when I was about halfway down the green. I turned to face the patio now some distance away but couldn't quite hear what she had said.

"I won't be long!" I trilled back though she probably couldn't hear me either. Turning on my heel and continuing on in the morning breeze.

I stepped through the large doors, the smell of hay and horses filling my nose. I was ashamed to say I hadn't been in here since long before I had left for America. My horse, Cinnamon, had died when I was 15 and I had refused to get another or even ride a horse ever since.

But now, being back I had an urge to learn again and maybe in time get another horse of my own. Perhaps Mr Taylor would be willing to teach me sometime. He was always very kind to me; he was the one who consoled me after the passing of my horse. And it was Mr Taylor who first taught me to ride a horse so I hoped he would replay his role of teacher. If not him, for I'm sure he is very busy, then a stable hand might be able to. Riding again would take up some of this free time I now found myself with and less free time was less time for my mother to berate me about finding a husband.

I looked around for Mr Taylor. When my eyes found no sign of him, I ventured further down the gangway. At the end of the rows of stalls the barn branched off to several back rooms and what looked like more stalls. I chose to go right where I could see a dim light down a hallway. Stepping up to the half-open door I gave two short knocks before making my entrance. The man, who was standing by a large old desk and turned to acknowledge me, was not Mr Taylor.

"Hi, can I help you?" Brief surprise flitted across his features as he looked at me. Whatever had caused his surprise didn't stop him from dragging his gaze down my body. I would have felt the need to be shy if I wasn't returning the favour. This man was dangerously good-looking. He was well built with muscles you could just see the definition of under his clothes. His button-up untucked, with the sleeves rolled to the elbow teasing strong forearms. Deep brown hair swept back from his forehead complimented his golden eyes. They were warm with a wicked glint in them, probably thanks to the cocky smile he was sporting.

Shaking off my momentary brain freeze I introduced myself. "Hi, I'm Miss Penhall or Natalie if you'd prefer." I thought of offering a handshake but settled on not.

"I know who you are, Miss Penhall," he replied coolly. Ah, so the smile wasn't a friendly one, noted.

"Oh." He hadn't offered his name, so I continued with my original mission. "I was actually looking for Mr Taylor."

"Well, you found him."

I stood bewildered before it clicked that this must be his son. I grasped for his name in my memories.

"Luke." He plainly stated solving my internal puzzling and looking slightly offended as he did so.

Right, Luke. We had played together a few times as kids, until one day when he just stopped wanting to hang out with me. We had been no more than ten but the rejection had stung. "Yes, sorry I do remember." I still tried to find some connection between the goofy boy I had known way back then, to the man in front of me now. "Sorry but is your father around?" This was starting to get awkward and the sooner I could find Mr Taylor Sr the better.

"No, he retired two years ago." He sounded bored of this interaction. His tone implying, I should have already known that information.

"I just got back yesterday. I've been away for a while." I tried to give an explanation for my ignorance. I shuffled uncomfortably under his never-ending gaze. "Now I'm back I was going to ask your dad for something." Trailing off I could see his disinterest growing.

"As I said he's not here so you might struggle." I frowned at his rude tone.

"Well, maybe you could help instead?" I tried to keep my tone polite and omit the irritation I was starting to feel.

"I doubt that I'm quite busy." Another brush-off. This was going nowhere.

"Oh, well I guess I'll leave you be then."

"OK."

I left the office and his sight quickly. Annoyed and put out I all but stomped back up the garden.

Back in the house, I made my way to the kitchen in search of a glass of water. Letting the tap run through until cold, the interaction with Luke kept replaying in my mind. He had been arrogant and rude, and I tried to remember more from before I left to see if I had offended him in some manner. I hadn't seen him in at least eight years and had not spoken for a further near decade prior to that, how was I supposed to recall his name at the drop of a hat? Or know he was Mr Taylor's son on sight, he looked far different to how I remember. Not that that was a bad thing. He was very attractive and something about those eyes made me feel things I certainly shouldn't be. No bad Natalie, he obviously doesn't think that highly of me. But he did check me out.

13

The idea had me blushing and I didn't like it. Stupid beautiful jerk.

Maria entering the kitchen interrupted my thoughts. "How did it go with Mr Taylor?" She asked innocently enough but I knew her better, a small smile hid at the corner of her mouth.

"That was not the Mr Taylor I was expecting to find, and I think you know that." I accused narrowing my eyes at her slightly.

She chuckled. "I did try to call you back to tell you."

"I couldn't hear you!" I protested not really cross at the woman but more at my impatient self.

"Well, I figured you'd soon find out for yourself, so no harm done." She moved around the kitchen putting things from breakfast away as she went.

"Actually, some harm done I made a complete idiot of myself and didn't even get what I went there for," I muttered pouting slightly.

"Oh dear." She covered her mouth to stifle another laugh. "I'm sure it'll be fine. Young Mr Taylor is so nice why didn't you just ask him, I'm sure he would have helped."

Nice was not the impression I got. I slumped into one of the seats at the island. "I tried! I'm not sure what you mean by nice but that is not how I would describe him."

"And how would you describe him dear?" She winked at me from across the kitchen.

"MARIA!" I scolded her, though she had hit the nail on the head. "He was just arrogant and rude, very stand-offish. Like he couldn't be bothered with me at all. Not that he needs to fawn over me, but he doesn't even really know me. Yet he dismissed me because he was 'too busy'. I mean what kind of ignorant arsehole won't even listen to someone who has come to them for help." I was still ranting when the mud-room door opened, and the man of the morning stepped into the kitchen. Oh poo. I bit my lip and wondered if running would be super obvious. He gave no indication that he heard me though.

"Morning Maria." He flashed a smile in her direction, one I didn't think he was capable of. It made him look even more handsome and angered me even more. So, it was just me he had decided to dislike. The housekeeper greeted him in a similarly friendly manner though she kept side-eyeing me. Oh no, I was not putting on a nice front for him. "I've got your veggies here and I've been told there is a boatload of rhubarb to be picked when you're happy for us to bring it up."

"Thank you, Luke, I'll let you know about the rhubarb." She patted his shoulder as she examined the trugg of vegetables. Luke looked over at me his mouth slightly opening like he was about to speak to me. "Did you want a cup of tea love?" Maria unknowingly interrupted whatever it was he was going to say.

"No, I best get back, thank you though." One more look at me and he was gone back through the door.

"See," I said as soon as I knew he would be out of earshot.

Maria sighed. "See what?"

"He's completely dismissive of me."

"Well, you didn't speak to him either." I went to protest and realised she was right. "Maybe just go and ask him what you wanted, otherwise you'll never get it." Again, she was right.

"Fine."

"Good Luck." The woman sing-songed as I left again for the barn.

Luke wasn't in the office. A couple of stable hands were there, and after a brief conversation, they pointed me in the direction of the tack room. It was in the other wing of the barn past a few isolated stalls. Seeing the door slightly open I knocked like before but decided to wait outside this time.

"Come in." A deep male voice spoke from inside the room.

Following orders, I entered the tack room my eyes going straight to Mr Taylor. He was stood over a work bench, a large chestnut saddle slung over it. The smell of leather was so strong in here that it almost blinded every other sense. His hands were working over the saddle with a cloth, an

16

open bottle of polish stood on the counter next to him. Raising his eyes, he regarded me with the same coolness as before. *Yeah, Maria, he's a real peach.*

"Oh, it's you." Was all he said before carrying on with his task.

"Um, yeah, it's me." *Five stars Natalie, I think we all know that.* "Listen I'm not sure how but we seem to have gotten off on the wrong foot. I apologise if I offended you in any way but that wasn't my intention."

"Which offence?" His reply was crisp but there was a hint of something on his face. An emotion I couldn't place.

"Uh, well...forgetting you...your name I mean. Earlier. You knew who I was, I forgot your name. It was rude and I am sorry."

He raised his eyebrows before heaving the saddle into his arms. "Is that all?" Slinging it over a high hanging stand his shirt rose as he lifted it from his arms. His lower abs exposed and as tanned and toned as the rest of him had me looking away trying to stifle my creeping blush.

"Well..." I had no idea what had gotten into me I was a bumbling mess, and he probably thought so too.

Taking a deep sigh, he crossed his arms and levelled me with his stare. "What do you want?"

"Huh?"

He rolled his eyes slightly. "Earlier. What did you want from my father?"

"Oh!" I was shocked he was even asking, maybe he was going to help me. "Riding lessons!" I blurted the statement sounding desperate. "I really want to learn to ride, not that I don't know how. It's just been a while."

A slow grin spread across his face. It didn't look friendly. "No." The word slapped all the enthusiasm out of me.

"No?" When my question went unanswered, I shrilled. "Why?!"

Shrugging he took a couple of steps towards me slow and purposeful. I'd have taken a few back myself had my feet not refused to move. My mind already deciding not to be intimidated by this grumpy man-child. "Don't want to."

"That's it?" I stared at him incredulously. "Fine. I'll ask someone else." I turned on heel to leave, maybe find those stable hands and see if any of them had the will to help me.

"Ah, that's not going to work."

Huffing I turned back to him. "And why not?"

"They're busy, I'm busy. Also, I'm sure you don't want to be taught by an ignorant arsehole anyway." His golden eyes should have been ice white with the coldness he was throwing out of them. A nasty victory smirk on his lips. If I had been embarrassed or felt guilty that he had heard me it passed quickly. This dick was not about to win this battle, so I pulled out the only weapon I had.

Lifting one shoulder in a half-shrug like I wasn't bubbling with anger I smiled back at him. "No matter I'll just ask my father to get someone to teach me." I hated using my status over people, it wasn't who I wanted to be, but this guy does work for us, and it was the only play in my hand.

"Ooh, except he will come to me to ask, and I'll tell him 'Sir, we simply don't have time, the racing season is all but here, and we have so much to do to get the horses ready. I am truly sorry maybe in autumn if the young miss would be willing to wait." I gaped at him.

"Why won't you help me?" I was defeated and tired of this tug of war. Dejected. My hopes of escaping from the house and my mother, even for a while, were all but gone.

"I believe I already explained why. I suppose it boils down to just not wanting to and just not liking you." He turned his back on me grabbing another saddle from the wall. "Why would I want to intentionally spend time with you or even help you?"

I felt a few hot angry tears prick at my eyes. *What an arsehole!* Not content for him to have the last stab I threw a final shot at his back before leaving. "Thank you for confirming my earlier assessment of you Mr Taylor."

It was still early, and the stables and grounds were relatively empty of people. I made it back to the house without anyone seeing the few angry tears I quickly swept away

19

with the back of my hand. Stepping through the French doors Maria was no longer in the kitchen. I thanked my luck as I don't think I could deal with the questions. Trudging through to the entryway meaning to run and hide in my room I nearly bumped into Lady Penhall. Surprised and quickly straightening my posture I greeted the immaculate Lady.

"Mother, when did you get back?"

"Only a few moments ago, I was coming looking for you actually." She regarded me. "I have something to discuss with you."

Yes, hello Mother.

My flight was fine thank you.

My room is lovely.

I am tired but glad to be home.

Answers to questions she didn't ask. I tried not to dwell on that, she had always been like this. Less mother more instructor. I didn't speak now though, I had nothing she wanted to hear.

"Tomorrow morning, we have a guest. I need you to look nice." She dragged her gaze down me, raised eyebrows sighting her disapproval at my casual attire. "A dress. Nice and simple. You need to look smart…" She paused once again looking me over. "You know what, I shall choose something for you. I will have it ready for the morning." I only nodded in response too tired and overwhelmed with the morning to argue. Satisfied I had understood, she nodded and left me standing alone in the hall.

3
Luke

I threw the saddle onto the bench with more force than it reasonably needed. When I heard Natalie was coming back, I didn't know what to think, now I do. I always thought her pretty, but she had grown into a beautiful woman in the time she had been away.

I remember when I first met her. She had been nine and I was ten. I had just started coming to work with my father. He was her riding coach at the time, so we saw a lot of each other. Back then she was more of a tomboy preferring to ride horses and traipse around the woods than play inside with her girlfriends. And for that summer she was my best friend.

I frowned slightly at the thought she couldn't even remember my name. Not that she should have to, maybe I'm remembering it differently. She probably had lots of friends and things to occupy her mind even at nine. She is the heir to the estate so I shouldn't reasonably expect her to. My most intact memory of that summer though is the day I told her I didn't want to be her friend anymore. I told my dad the night before how much I liked her, OK maybe I had a little crush, but she really was a great friend. He gave my mum a look before taking me to one side. Telling me I couldn't be friends with Natalie. I got angry and argued. He told me it was for the best and that I had to be professional to do this job. I didn't fully understand what he meant but I wanted to be like my dad so much that I did as he asked.

The next day when Natalie came up to me asking me to go play I did it. In the clumsy ill-worded way of a ten-year-old. But it worked all the same, she started crying and ran off. I wanted to say sorry, I didn't want to make my friend upset. She didn't talk to me again, until today. I had seen her around as we both grew up, but our paths never crossed. To begin with, I think she avoided me on purpose, but then after her pony died and her duties became more involved, it just happened to be that we were never in the same spaces.

It made sense to me now, what my dad asked of me. He squashed a crush that he saw even before I had a name on it. He knew it would only end badly for both Nat and I so he put a stop to it. I couldn't resent him for that. And I was over that schoolboy crush, or I thought I was. When she stepped into my office this morning, I knew immediately who she was. I smiled now remembering how she checked me out, not that I wasn't doing the same. I couldn't deny she was beautiful. Standing in front of me her clothes hugging her slight curves, soft pink lips with a heart-breaking smile on them. Her eyes were golden, and I could see the lust in them as she roamed them over me. I grinned pleased to know she liked what she saw. I felt heat spread through me and my heart rate sped up. Stopping that feeling I listened as she fumbled on about needing to speak to my dad. It irritated me so much that she had no idea who I was, or even that my dad had retired years ago. I let spite take over, I don't know why I chose to be mean to her, but it was

23

a far better feeling than trying to suppress the thoughts I was having.

Thoughts that now played freely while I roughly oiled the saddle. Why did she have to be so friendly? I mean even after I was rude to her, she still came back and apologised. How insufferable. I had gotten under her skin though, telling her I didn't want to teach her because I didn't like her had been a lie. She backed off and that is exactly what I needed. Just like when I was ten there was danger in getting too close to her. Having her hate me was the safest option, and it seemed I achieved that. Not that I felt overly good about it.

Going back to my office I found it occupied. Great. I like the guys that work for me but right now I needed head space. Adrenaline still high from arguing with her and the unshakeable image of her smile in my brain. Get yourself together Luke.

"Boss."

"Tea?"

The lads greeted me, I waved off the offer sitting in the chair at my desk. They continued their conversation unbothered by my presence. My office always doubled as a sort of staff room, especially for the lads working in the stables.

"Did you see her though?" Their talk caught my attention, but I didn't raise my head from my work.

"Yeah, mate I'm not blind."

"Wonder if she'll be coming down to ride at all?"

"Probably, this is her stables."

"It's her dad's."

"Same thing."

I bit my tongue trying not to show any interest.

"I'll teach her to ride if she likes." Dan one of the more arrogant lads chimed in. I placed my pen down anger nudging at me to react. "Hey boss, did the lady want some lessons? I would like to be first to put my name in the hat." He laughed, and a couple of the others snorted.

"Enough." My own voice cut through their banter, colder than I expected but I didn't apologise. I looked between them all then landed my eyes on Dan. He was still smiling slightly. Dick. "She's your boss, I will have no talk like that. I assume you all like your positions here?" I took the silence as confirmation. "You'll even get to keep them if you stop perving over Miss Penhall. I won't have you calling me or the work the rest of us do here into question. Imagine if someone hears you and tells his Lordship. We would all be out, myself included for allowing it. I'm not throwing hard work away so you can turn Miss Penhall into a fetish." What I said was true, they walked a shaky line talking freely about Lord Byron's daughter like that. I would be lying if I said that was my only reason for calling them out. How they spoke of Natalie made my blood boil and I was

25

trying very hard to stop from punching Dan in his stupid face.

They didn't look offended just a little guilty. Throwing out a few mumbled apologies and excuses. Dan quickly trying to retract his statement. "I was just joking boss, didn't mean anything by it." I nodded slightly.

"Well, you've all been warned, and you only get one." I needed to lighten the mood and get them out of my office. "Bugger off and do something, the lot of you. Mike, we need to discuss stock."

They all left, bar Mike who sat in the chair opposite pulling out the stock sheets and beginning to go through them. I tried to pay attention and not let my mind be filled with the thought of brown eyes and a sweet smile.

4
Natalie

True to her word my mother had planned my outfit and it was in my room ready in the morning. Beige and boring. Sorry, 'neutral and classy'. The dress, which hung from a hook in my wardrobe, was not my style. It was by no means ugly but not something I would choose. I sighed readying myself with what she had prepared and behaving myself by choosing appropriate matching items. Thirty minutes later I stood looking at myself in a beige dress, beige shoes and beige makeup. I looked older and duller. I tried to smile convincingly at myself before heading downstairs. If I could make it look half real to me maybe it would fool the rest of them.

Descending the staircase, I saw my mother standing in the foyer with a man next to her. He was tall with very dark hair and dressed in an immaculate suit. They both turned to acknowledge my presence and I got my first full look at his face. He was handsome, and conventionally well put together. A meticulously groomed man with not a hair out of place. No detail left unplanned. Sharp brows (definitely plucked), which he raised at my appearance. The image of a certain dishevelled grounds manager snapped into my head and was quickly escorted out as I took the last few steps.

Without speaking a word of greeting my mother introduced me to the man. "Mr Layton this is my daughter, Natalie, isn't she beautiful?" She half-whispered that last comment to him, in that stupid volume people do when they know full well everyone can still hear them. He dragged his eyes down me, this felt worlds different from when Luke had done the same thing not 24 hours previous. The lecherous look in his eyes made me want to cover myself up, though what I was wearing was entirely modest. He grasped my hand, and placed a kiss to the back of it, looking at me through his lashes as he did so.

"An absolute pleasure to meet you, Miss Penhall, you can call me Peter." He straightened before continuing his evaluation of my body.

"You too, Peter." I tried to be polite, but my bewilderment must have played through the facade as my mother interrupted our greeting.

"We are just waiting for your father and then we can discuss the details."

"I'm sorry, discuss what?" I looked straight at my mother now showing clear confusion with what she was talking about. I saw Mr Layton look slightly taken aback and skew his eyes from me to Lady Penhall also.

"The terms of your engagement Natalie what else," She spoke as if I was somehow aware of this already. I tried to remain calm, but in my mind, I couldn't believe she had moved so fast. I had not been back three days, and this is what she does. Before I could go into full-blown panic mode Lord Penhall made his arrival. My father looked at the three of us before heading towards his office.

"Shall we?" He asked no one in particular knowing we would all follow anyway. Peter and my mother moved to follow him.

"I'll join you in just a moment." The words moved on their own and my mother gave me a tight-lipped smile. She could hardly protest loudly in front of guests, so she simply nodded.
I walked swiftly into the kitchen and shut the door, leaning over the island I tried to calm myself. This was not happening. I couldn't believe I hadn't figured out what she was up to, but then I was more shocked that she didn't think I needed to know that information. I mean maybe she thought I would wiggle my way out of this meeting. She wasn't wrong. If I had known, I would have at least tried to delay this. I had only spoken one sentence to him, but I already didn't like what I saw.

I knew he would be my mother's choice, but she doesn't seem to have taken me into consideration at all. And it's fairly obvious what's on his mind. My skin started to crawl at the memory of his wandering eyes. It was exactly the feeling I wanted to avoid. Like a prize cow. Someone who could be bought, someone who could be sold.

"You OK there?" I jumped a mile at the voice. Luke stood at the other end of the island a bag in his hand which he placed on the counter. He looked concerned or maybe he thought I was crazy, either way, I couldn't deal with him today.

29

"I'm fine." I stood up straight and made my features neutral. He didn't look convinced; in fact, the concern was starting to look a lot more like he thought I was crazy. I nodded politely at him and left for my father's office. This wasn't going away so I might as well face the music. Maybe Peter wouldn't be as bad as his first impression.

All conversation halted when I entered, the room falling suspiciously quiet. My father sat at his desk wearing the same unreadable expression. My mother sat on one of the chairs her expression the complete opposite, a beaming smile and a hidden warning in her eyes. Neither of them held my attention though. Peter had turned in his seat to stare at me. A disturbing pitying look on his face.

"Hey there." His tone was like that you used on a nervous child, feather soft and condescending to anyone over the age of four. "Your father and mother were just explaining to me that you aren't too keen on the idea of marrying someone you don't know." I wanted to roll my eyes and laugh but he wasn't finished. "I completely understand how it could be very scary, but I think if you get to know me, you'll see I'm a nice guy." He said the last part patting the seat next to him.

I don't know if it was the infuriating tone he was using, the 'nice guy' cliché or the way he patted the seat like I needed help finding it. Either way, I was certain no matter how much I got to know this guy, I would never like the idea of marrying him. I sat in the seat all the same ignoring the triumphant looks of Peter and my mother.

What followed was the most awkward meeting or I suppose chaperoned first date in history. Peter asked about my time in the States and my hobbies, he feigned interest in my replies. I returned the questions and the courtesy of feigning interest in his words. Is this what arranged marriage is like? Is this what my parents have? The rest of the meeting passed by painfully slowly, probably not helped by my refusal to discuss anything remotely wedding related, and my sitting mute when the others felt the need to. My mother finally escorted Mr Layton to the door, not before another icky back-of-the-hand kiss. Finally alone with my father, I wasted no time.

"You can't be serious?" I levelled him with a stare waiting for him to agree that Peter was an awful choice.

"Natalie," He sighed running a hand through his pepper hair. "Please don't start, you have known your whole life that this would happen."

"Don't start? I don't know where to start. It's one thing to expect an arranged marriage it is entirely another to move halfway across the world to be welcomed home by that! We have nothing in common and I have seen pieces of cardboard with a more interesting character." I tried to not raise my voice. "I just don't understand why?"

Lord Penhall though had seemingly had enough "Because it is family tradition Natalie, because you are part of this family and because it is what is best. Mr Layton is a perfectly respectable man, and you will accept him as your husband." He had his look of authority on. He wasn't going to budge on this.

"So you're saying I have no choice?"

"For goodness' sake girl don't be so dramatic, it's hardly a burden to marry a rich, handsome man, is it?"

I wasn't winning this battle. But maybe I could make use of the irritation I had caused my father. "I guess it's just a huge change for me." I tried a different approach; I needed at least one win today. "Moving back, a new fiancé I guess I just need something to take my mind off of things."

"What is it that you want?" He always knew when I was hinting at something. And right now, I'd bet he would do anything to get rid of me.

"Riding lessons."

"Mr Taylor…" He began but I interrupted.

"Has already told me no. He said they are too busy with the racing season." I pouted slightly still put out a little at the rebuff yesterday.

"Well, there you have it. That man knows what he's talking about and if he says they don't have time he has my trust that that's the truth." He picked up some papers on his desk and I briefly considered retelling Luke and my interaction.

Deciding it wouldn't be worth it I tried a different angle. "Maybe we could hire a tutor. It could even be in-house if you know anyone that would do it. On their time with pay obviously so as not to interrupt Mr Taylor's important schedule." I masked the sarcasm in that last part.

My father thought for a moment before answering. "We have a young man working for us. Charlie. He's a good rider and a good coach so I've heard. Offer him full pay for teaching you. In his own time."

I clasped my hands together and squeaked, my father winced. "Thank you, thank you, thank you." He waved off my excitement signalling me to leave him but not before I caught the small smile at the edge of his mouth.

"Charlie?" I asked the young man who was ankle-deep in hay. He raised his head of blonde hair to meet my eye. He was 21 so a few years my junior but if my father was right, he was the man I needed. A thin layer of sweat shined on his brow. The day was hot, and the barn was somehow hotter still.

"Yes, Miss?" He confirmed.

"Nice to meet you, I'm Natalie and I have a question for you if you have the time?" I stood back allowing him out of the stall. He wiped his hands on a rag from the wooden door and nodded at me to continue. "Um, so I need someone to teach me to ride or re-teach me. I kind of just need a refresher lesson or two but I'm not entirely hopeless at it or I wasn't anyway." I stopped realising I was rambling. He smiled at me with amusement.

33

"What I'm trying miserably to ask is will you teach me?" I chewed my lip nervously I wanted to learn so badly and I wasn't sure he would agree to help me.

"Oh, well I suppose I could though I'll just check with Luke, Mr Taylor..."

"No." I cut him off, admittedly probably too quickly as he seemed a little taken aback. "Sorry, what I mean is I spoke to Luke already and he said he doesn't have the time, and that none of his staff could spare the time either."

"But you still want me to help you? I'm sorry Miss I haven't been here long, and I don't want to make waves with the boss man. Are you sure you want ME to teach you?" He looked sceptical and I couldn't blame him, his boss had already spoken on the matter and here I was seemingly trying to get him into trouble.

"Yes?" I grinned at him "Besides Luke refusing to teach me, I do think you are the best person for the task. My father speaks very highly of you and says you've been riding as long as you can walk. I'm convinced what you can't teach me about riding isn't worth my knowing."

He nodded smiling slightly at the praise. Rubbing the back of his neck he considered it for a moment. "I'm sorry Miss Penhall but my life wouldn't be worth it if I go against Luke. Not least from the other guys, he has a lot of respect from them and I'm still the new kid." He began to walk away pausing briefly. "I really am sorry." I wasn't giving up so easily.

"What if it's overtime?" I called down the walkway after him. He stopped turning on his heel. I took that as my cue to continue. "Lord Penhall has authorised fair payment to teach me. As a private lesson. Within your own time. With a separate fee so no chance of getting in trouble with 'Boss Man'." He stared at me, maybe making sure I was serious or weighing the risk vs reward. "Only if you would be happy to help me in your time off, I know I'm asking a lot, but I'd rather be taught by someone that knows the horses than some random instructor. I'd be forever in your debt. You'd be the bestest ever." He started laughing at that last bit holding his hand up.

"You can stop, I kind of wanted to do it anyway, it'll be fun to teach someone. Plus, you've given me a get-out-of-jail card with Luke so it's all good... Also, who says bestest?" He raised a brow still amused at my begging.

"I do when I'm trying to convince the bestest to teach me!" I jibed back. "But seriously thank you." He waved it off.

"I'm off tomorrow unless that's no good?"

"No tomorrow will be perfect what time?"

"Be down here." He pointed at the ground between us. "At say, 9.30?"

"Sounds good, I'll see you tomorrow, Bestest." I heard him laughing a little as I left.

5
Natalie

The next morning, I arrived at that spot in the barn at 9.28. I shifted nervously in my riding boots, trying to smooth my sweaty hands off on my jodhpurs. Trying to calm myself, I'm not entirely sure why I was so nervous, it had been a while, yes, but I always loved riding. It shouldn't be too difficult to get back into it. I couldn't be more thankful to Charlie for helping me, I felt this is what I needed to maintain some normality and peace at the moment. And with Luke being more than horrible about the whole thing I was relieved I was able to persuade him. Footsteps caused me to turn my head in the direction of the back of the barn. Charlie was briskly walking towards me a smile on his face.

"Are we ready?" He beamed at me with a lot of enthusiasm for a guy up early on his day off.

"Mhm," I managed to hum a confirmation.

"Nervous?" He raised a brow as we walked towards a stall.

I let out a nervous laugh. "A little."

"Don't be, you'll be great. And you're being taught by the 'Bestest' after all." I laughed less nervously this time.

"Glad to hear you're adopting the nickname."

"I figured you are in charge, so you must be right. Might as well own it." He shrugged giving me a goofy grin. Shaking my head, I followed him to ready our horses.

45 minutes later I was leading 'Toby', an older horse from the stables. Charlie was following with a younger mare called 'Opal' on the end of his lead rope. Tacking had taken a little longer than usual as Charlie wanted to go through everything with me. Although he joked that 'A lady such as myself will always have mere mortals to do it for her, she should still know how to do it herself." He earned himself a shove and eye roll for the first comment. Stopping next to me he watched as I mounted the horse and then adjusted my stirrups on both sides until he was satisfied I was secured enough.

He swiftly mounted his own horse and turned to me. "You doing ok?" I nodded at him, Toby was a large horse, and it would take getting used to being up so high again but I wasn't as nervous as I thought I would be. "Good, seeing as it's still sweltering today, I thought a tack through the woods would be best. For us and the horses, it's a good idea to keep to the shade as much as possible." He looked to me for confirmation again.

"Sounds good to me." He wasn't wrong about the heat; any shade he was offering I was game for.

"If you want to stop at any point, let me know and we can take a break or head back." He clicked his tongue pressing his heel into Opal to get her to walk on. I did the same with

Toby and the old boy dutifully followed the mare. The pair walked into the verge of the woods lining the property. Several paths well worn by horses and people webbed through the trees and Charlie picked one, setting off into the cool welcome of the shaded woodland. We walked, trotted and talked for most of the morning. I found myself immensely enjoying the experience. Charlie was the most normal company I had had since my return. I could just chat with him like I was out meeting a friend, albeit one that was being paid to be there. But I didn't mind the horse riding was worth every penny and the company was a very welcome bonus. He asked me about my time in America and I asked how he got into horse riding and then landed this job. My father hadn't been exaggerating when he boasted of Charlie's experience, he had practically spent his whole life in the saddle of a horse. Now working here, he was tasked with training up some of our racing and show horses.

The day passed by too quickly and before I knew it, we were breaking the tree line. "There is no way your dad didn't know it was you!" I laughed at his story half gobsmacked at his antics and the other half really not surprised at what he used to get up to. He was every inch the cheeky, always getting-into-trouble lad.

"I swear he didn't find out! Or maybe he did but he never let on!" He was laughing too.

"That seems more likely, you probably gave it away laughing." The horses' hooves on the stone courtyard punctuated our conversation.

"He did use to tell me that I had a certain smile and glint in my eye when I was up to no good."

"Aha, I told you they always know, take it from someone that got away with absolutely nothing!"

"I'm sure you found a way to not do as you were told!"

"Yes, you're right, but I always got caught in the end!"

We put the horses away after giving them a well-earned brush down and drink. I made sure to thank Toby for being so gentle with me and promised to visit him with some carrots. Exiting the stables, we sat together on one of the benches in the shade of the barn.

"Would you like another lesson then?" Charlie asked looking at me.

"Absolutely! I enjoyed today and to be honest I think now that the nerves and anxiety are out of the way I could do a bit more next time. I used to be able to at least do novice jumping, and not that I expect Toby would be game for that I would like to keep training until I get a horse or the confidence to do that again." He nodded along with what I was saying.

"I think that is entirely possible with a few more lessons."

"Good, I had a lot of fun so I don't think I would complain about doing it again. That is as long as you don't mind it is your day off after all."

He pulled a face his mouth setting into a line. "It was tough going to be honest, but I can't argue with extra money so I guess I could endure a few more lessons." I frowned but I guess I understood.

"Only if you're sure I know you would probably rather do something else, but I do appreciate it." I looked at the yard before hearing a laugh beside me. Charlie's face was back to its usual cheeky grin.

"Oh my god, I'm joking Nat! Jesus, I didn't think you would believe me so readily! Today's been fun I liked it regardless of the money!" I scowled at him but couldn't keep up my anger, breaking into a laugh with him. I shoved his arm hard enough to make him rock but not fall on the bench.

"That was not very nice! I really panicked!"

"Sorry, sorry, I couldn't help myself!" He surrendered. I was still laughing when he suddenly sobered. Looking over my shoulder I couldn't help but follow his eye line. Luke was storming across the yard towards us, he looked pissed.

"Uh oh here comes grumpy." I teased; Charlie cracked a grin, but it didn't sway the worry in his eyes.

"Luke." He addressed him as he stopped in front of us. Luke crossed his arms and raised a brow looking between the pair of us.

"What's going on?"

I wasn't sure who he was talking to, so I decided to answer for both of us. "None of your business." He snapped his gaze to me, and I swear I could see steam coming out of his ears. I had to bite my lip to stop from smirking, I didn't think it would help either of us right now.

"The hell it's not I was just told that you took two horses out this morning." That was directed at Charlie, who looked calm but concerned. "I thought I said my staff couldn't spare the time. In fact, I was quite explicit that none of them had the time." That was aimed at me. Both Charlie and I were standing now facing our unwelcome interruption.

"Luke I'm not..." Charlie started.

"Not what? Working? Correct you're not, you're wasting time taking country rides and flirting. You aren't paid for either."

I wasn't having him talk to Charlie like that after how much he had helped me and lifted my spirits. "Except 'Boss man' he's not on your time, it's his day off! Lord Penhall is paying him to teach me, so you can stop speaking to him like that." I pointed my finger at Luke's chest. "IF you have an issue with what the staff of this house do in their spare time then I suggest you take it up with my father!" He looked thrown for a moment but undeterred.

"It didn't look like he was doing much teaching I'm wondering what your dad would say about that. I'm sure this isn't how he wanted his money spent!" He looked between the pair of us. Charlie's eyes never left Luke.

41

"Who do you think you're talking..." Charlie put his hands on my shoulders and steered me away.

"It's OK Nat, I'll sort it."

"But?"

He silenced me again. "Honestly it'll be fine." I sighed giving up, I didn't want to ruin this day any more than Luke had so I lamented.

"Fine." He smiled slightly at my pout. I looked at Luke, then back to Charlie. "Let me know if you still want to teach me, but I understand if not."

"I do, give me your number I'll text you some days I'm free." I did as Charlie asked reading out my number and waiting for his text so I could save his. The whole time Luke stood there seething; it would have been comical if he wasn't being such an arse as usual.

"Got it, you're saved as 'Bestest'." I smiled; Luke scoffed. "Good luck" I muttered before escaping up the hill to the house. I turned briefly to see the two men in discussion heading back into the stables. I hoped Luke wouldn't be too hard on him. He could be nasty and I didn't want Charlie in hot water because of me.

It was late in the evening before I heard from Charlie. A text pinged through just as I was settling on the sofa in my room.

Hey, I know it's late but wanted to let you know I'm off next week on Wednesday and Friday. Can do either or both if you are keen. C.

Hi, that's OK thanks for messaging. Next Wednesday is good for me. Not sure about Friday can I let you know in the morning? N. P.S. Have you still got a head or was it bitten off?

Sure. Yeah, it's still there though not for lack of trying. He calmed down after I told him I would still be teaching you and that was that. C.

I'm sorry to put you in that position but also, I'm glad you're still game so maybe not too sorry. N.

Wow! You're a bad friend.

You thought we were friends?

Double wow!

Joking! Goodnight.

Night.

6
Natalie

The following Wednesday I met with Charlie at 9.30, same
spot. Just as before I arrived first. I leaned on one of the
stalls considerably less nervous than the last lesson. My
excitement now outweighing any remaining nerves. I
scrolled through my phone while I waited, uninterested in
what I saw but liking a few posts from distant friends all the
same. Hearing people talking I slid the phone back into my
jacket pocket and pushed myself off the stall door. I smiled
down the barn as Charlie came out of the office until I saw
whom he was talking to. Luke walked next to him. He was
dressed like something out of a Hollywood cowboy film, all
denim jeans and check shirts. And as with every time our
paths cross, I considered how much of a shame it was that
someone so good-looking was such an arse. Imagine how
cute he'd be if he stopped being so grumpy.

Thankfully Luke didn't catch me staring, but Charlie did.
He tried to hide a smile; I just narrowed my eyes in
response. His light laughter at my reaction finally drawing
Luke's gaze to me. Now only a few feet away he smiled
sweetly and so very unlike himself. "Miss Penhall."
Greeting me he crossed his arms the rolled sleeves of his
shirt protesting against his tanned biceps.

"Mr Taylor," I replied neither sweetly nor with disdain. I turned my attention to Charlie. The young man had been watching our introduction with amusement. "Are you re…"

I couldn't finish my sentence as Luke spoke again. "How have you been?" I sighed quietly looking back at him.

"Fine. You?" He was still smiling sweetly but the slight condescending in his tone and the mischief in his eyes betrayed his expression. He was trying to wind me up.

"Do you know what?" He looked around. "I'm doing great. Pretty hectic week but as I'm sure you'll be pleased to hear it's all going well. Obviously, you'll be in charge one day so I'm happy to show you some numbers if you like."

I pursed my lips trying not to take the bait. Charlie was looking at Luke like he had lost the plot having not been privy to Luke and I's previous exchanges. When I realised he was waiting for an answer I responded to the overly enthusiastic charade. "Sounds great, I'll find some time in my schedule and let you know." I again turned to Charlie begging he would dismiss us from this ridiculous conversation. Luke clicked his fingers making me start.

"I know! I can come with you today!" I simmered turning to look at him. His sweet smile fully gone now replaced with the arrogant, mean smirk he usually wears for me. "Two teachers are better than one right?"

He thought he got me, and for a moment so did I. I pasted a smile on my face like I didn't have a care in the world.

45

"No." I paused letting the single word sink into him. "Thank you though. When you have the Bestest, one teacher is all you need. Also, I know you're super busy and don't have time to teach me so we will be OK on our own." I decided not to wait for Charlie any more and made my own way towards Toby's stall. He followed me laughing as he jogged slightly to catch up.

"That was interesting." I could feel Charlie looking at me but I kept my gaze forward.

"What was?" I replied.

"That whole thing." He waved a hand behind us.

"I don't know what you're talking about." Truth be told that was one of the more normal conversations I'd had with Luke, and it felt weird. It annoyed me somewhat that once again Luke had to try and ruin what was currently the best thing I had.

"Well, the look on his face was brilliant when you rejected his offer."

This time I did look at him. "Did he look cross?"

"Furious."

"Good, serves him right." We both chuckled a little. "Honestly though I don't know what I did to make him so rude and childish towards me, so I figure he deserves to feel a little put-out."

"You don't know what you did," He said more to himself than me and I could see the smirk he was hiding.

"No…" I drew the word out narrowing my eyes. "But I get the impression you do. What did I do?"

"Oh no, you are not putting me in the middle of this if you want to know so bad you'll have to ask him yourself."

I huffed. "Does it look like that's an option?"

"Then you'll never know." He shrugged.

"That's mean." I poked my tongue out in a very charming manner.

"Now who's childish." He teased but revealed no more on the topic.

I only grumbled in response before saddling Toby.

We were heading back to the stables several hours later passing through one of the outer paddocks. It was full of wildflowers and long grass, currently uninhabited by anything. I pulled the large horse to a halt.

"I'm going to stay here for a bit. You can join me if you have nowhere to be." Calling to Charlie, I dismounted letting Toby wander to graze.

"I'm in no rush," He stated also dismounting. I smiled at him before dropping onto the grass. Stretching out I absent-mindedly pulled at the daises sprouted around me. Picking a spot next to me Charlie also sat down.

"Thanks for sitting with me. I didn't fancy heading back just yet."

"I thought you might want more than just riding lessons when you asked me to do this," He spoke knowingly.

I gaped at him. "W-what do you mean, I only asked you because Luke wouldn't let me. I wasn't trying to...this is just…"

"Natalie." He stopped me. "I meant you probably wanted some time to yourself. Away from everyone else." He side-eyed me. "But you picked me because I'm the best looking right?"

I tutted throwing a beheaded flower at him. "Dream on."

"Who are you avoiding?" He asked sobering a little.

"Less of a who more of a what."

"OK...what are you avoiding?"

"Everything." I laughed a little. "Sorry I shouldn't whinge; you're probably wondering what could possibly be wrong with my life.

"Ah everyone's got stuff they have to deal with. I bet you have your fair share."

"I guess I do. I think what's getting to me at the moment is the loneliness in it all. I have so much I want to talk about but everyone I know who would be on my side is being paid to talk to me." I winced. "Sorry," I added the apology realising I had lumped him in with that statement.

"I mean it's true I'm being paid right now but it doesn't mean you can't talk to me." I hesitated at what he said. "We can meet up when I'm not being paid you know."

"I meant it when I said I didn't hire you for *those* reasons." I teased him.

"If I wasn't so self-confident, I might be offended. I wasn't asking as a date. I'm asking as a friend. You know grab a pint, whinge about our lives. Be a mere mortal for a night."

I sat up from my slightly recline. "You know what, yeah, I'd like that. Friday?"

"Aren't you busy?"

"I am in the day, but I should be done by about 4 pm."

"Great so say meet at seven and go to The George?" He asked.

"Sounds like a plan," I confirmed.

I dragged myself out of bed the next morning. I had been awake for five minutes and was already in a foul mood. Mainly because I remembered I was having breakfast with Mr Layton today. I quickly dressed; it was pretty warm for May even at this hour. Making my way downstairs I trudged to the kitchen. Maria was already in there, the island covered in cloches I assumed hiding breakfast. I scowled at them. She regarded me with a pitying look, I had only obviously confided in her what I thought of Mr Layton, and she knew the last place I wanted to be was having this breakfast.

"Wendy has made a lovely spread for you this morning." She tried to sound cheery, showing a few of the dishes that our chef had prepared. It did lift my spirits slightly. Wendy wasn't with us every day, there wasn't much need a lot of the time, but she is absolutely fantastic. My stomach rumbled in anticipation. "I thought you could eat on the patio?" I only nodded in response, flopping down onto the nearest chair. No sooner had my butt hit the seat, than the doorbell sounded. "That'll be him."

"Urghh..." I protested standing back up. OK, smile Natalie. It might not be so bad, maybe I should at least give him a chance. I wasn't convincing myself, but I had to hold out hope.

"Mr Layton, so nice to see you." I hear Maria's charming voice in the foyer greeting my guest. She should go into acting.

50

They appeared in the kitchen doorway. Mr Layton wasted no time in approaching me and placing a kiss on the back of my hand. I tried to keep the frown from my face. Why must he keep doing that?

"Miss Penhall, you look beautiful this morning." He gazed up at me from his stooped position.

"Thank you, Mr Layton." I paused looking around, Maria met me eye nodding her head to the French doors. "Shall we eat on the patio this morning; it is such a nice day it would be a shame to waste the good weather."

"Excellent idea." He didn't release my hand instead hooking it through his arm and leading us outside. He pulled my seat out first waiting for me to take it before seating himself. Maria came out with a cloche in hand lifting it ceremoniously as she put it down revealing various pastries. I placed a croissant on my plate and didn't miss the expression on Mr Layton's face when I also reached for a pain au chocolat. He didn't comment. Smart boy.

"So, how have you been?" Lame but it was the only conversation starter I could think of to break this awkward silence.

"I've been well, business has been hectic but that's always a good thing." I didn't ask which of his businesses he was referring to. I couldn't remember all of them and certainly didn't want a revision on the topic.

"Hectic is good." I amiably agreed. The silence fell again.

51

A beat too long later he asked. "Are you well?" Mr Layton, that felt a little forced.

"I am thank you." I sipped my tea. "I've recently started horse riding again, so I've been keeping occupied."

"That's good." More silence. This meal was going to drag on forever at this rate. "Maybe after breakfast, you could give me a small tour of the grounds." He looked slightly out of his depth which I imagine for a man like him was rare.

"Of course, it would be my pleasure." I'd have felt pity for his discomfort if he wasn't alternating his attention between my eyes and my breasts. We finished our food without further conversation.

I began the tour of the grounds with the small hedge maze and fountain area, it held a beautiful view of the house. Its true splendour on full display from the water feature. I gave a small history of the manor to him, all the while he looked at the building with an odd smile on his face. It wasn't one of amazement, more satisfaction. Like the way you might look at a trophy you had won or an art piece, you had done yourself. He looked at my home as if it were an achievement of his. I didn't like it.

I offered to show him the stables next, I knew from our first meeting that he was fond of the races so I figured it would be of great interest to him. The walk down to them was brief and I kept a pace of distance between us in case he decided to loop my arm through his again.

Inside and outside the stables I showed him several of the horses we had reared, and it was the first time I had seen him genuinely impressed. He tried to scrutinise, I could see it in his face, but his efforts on finding fault were left wanting. We had good stock here, always had.

I was just finishing up the tour of the inside stalls when we bumped into Luke, coming out of his office. His eyes dropped down my summer dress caressing my bare legs, and as always, I felt myself warming under his gaze. His eyes came back to mine. "Good morning, Miss Penhall." All smiles and pleasantries for me today.

"Good morning Mr Taylor, I was just giving a tour of the stables to…" I didn't get to finish as Peter interrupted the friendly exchange.

His tone was very different from when we spoke. It was clipped and serious. "Mr Layton." He shook Luke's hand before slinging his arm around my waist. "Miss Penhall's fiancé."

I couldn't decide if the arm around me, or the fact he felt comfortable calling himself my fiancé shocked me more. For the briefest of moments something changed in Luke's friendly demeanour his eyes flicking to the hand at my hip. He composed quickly smiling, though this one was not sincere. "Nice to meet you."

"So, what do you do here Mr…" Peter trailed off.

"Taylor." Luke finished for him, everyone knowing he couldn't have forgotten his name in the last 30 seconds.

"I'm the grounds manager of the estate." He spoke with pride that made my heart happy and a small smile spread on my lips.

"Ah, I see." Was that slight intimidation I saw on Peter's face? "Well then, we best not keep you, you must be very busy. Besides me and Natalie have many plans for the day." He squeezed me a little closer and I struggled to keep the discomfort from showing.

"Enjoy the rest of your day." Friendly Luke had well and truly left, the cold sharp-tongued man I knew standing in his place. I nodded but said nothing as Peter led me away.

7
Luke

I stared at the pair of retreating frames for longer than I would pridefully admit to. A fiancé? She was engaged. She'd only been back what a week? And she was already engaged. Maybe it was a long-standing betrothal. But I had never seen or even heard of this Mr Layton before. He was a right tosser as well; I didn't miss the turned-up nose as he looked at me. If he was going to be Lord here, then I didn't see myself getting on with him like Lord Penhall.

Around midday Charlie found me sitting at my desk where I had hidden myself for the past few hours. He made himself a cup of tea before sipping it looking at me opening and closing his mouth like a fish.

"Spit it out," I demanded sick of watching him flounder and being in too bad a mood to entertain him.

"You super busy tomorrow?" He asked me, still not being direct.

"I'm always busy." I sighed seeing he wasn't going to just tell me. "What do you need Charlie?"

"To take Nat, I mean Miss Penhall's riding lesson." His response caught me off guard.

"Why?" I sounded short-tempered, but I couldn't deny my curiosity.

"She said she was busy tomorrow but turns out those plans got cancelled and she wanted the lesson. Only now I've promised my parents to help them out so I can't. I know you two don't get on all the time, but I don't want to let her down." He paused before adding. "I get it if not, just no one else who would be a good instructor is around."

"I'll do it." I found myself saying the words before I had fully decided I wanted to. I partly wanted to keep my word, that I was far too busy to entertain her lessons. But I wanted to see her more. It had bothered me all morning and I had to know where this fiancé had appeared from.

Charlie looked shocked at my response but didn't question my motives thankfully. "Great I'll let her know it's sorted then." He turned to leave but I stopped him.

"She'll probably cancel once she knows it's me anyway," I spoke trying to sound indifferent but also slightly disappointed that that was the most likely outcome.

He shrugged in return. "Nah, she'll show. I'll tell her 9.30. Thanks again boss." He left to make his arrangements and I went back to my paperwork. Though it was far less thought-consuming now I knew I would be spending the day with Natalie tomorrow. My plan to keep my distance was quickly going down the drain.

I had already been at the stables for over two hours when 9.30 rolled around. It had been a long couple of hours, my nerves on whether or not she would show up taking up most of the time. I was loitering in the gangway when she came in. As always she looked beautiful, my heart sped up a little as she looked at me. I didn't even mind that she looked more confused than happy.

"Where's Charlie?" Her soft voice asked. So he hadn't told her I would be taking the lesson. No wonder she showed up.

"Oh, um, didn't he tell you I'm taking your lesson today." I tried to hide the nerves, hoping I came across as nonchalant.

"No you're not." She looked like she didn't believe me, her eyes flicking around as if Charlie might jump out at any moment yelling 'Gotcha'.

I laughed lightly. "I am."

"No thank you." She turned on her heel beginning to walk away.

"Wait." I grasped her wrist, releasing it immediately when she looked down at my offending hand. "Sorry, but I'm here, you're here, why not just take the lesson?"

"Because you're always horrible to me and have admitted you don't like me." She crossed her arms. "So why would I?"

"I'm sure I can be nice for a few hours." I tempted her, she didn't look convinced. "Nice-ish?" I gave her a joking grin.

The corner of her mouth twitched a little. Rolling her eyes. "Fine. But you need to be the poster boy of 'nice-ish' or I'll turn Toby around and come back."

I held my hands up "Deal."

We set off through the woods, my plan was for a ride around the lakes set far from the property. Toby trotted a few paces behind, Natalie not saying anything. I slowed until we were side by side. She looked at me holding my gaze for a moment before looking away, back at the trail we were following.

"What was America like then?" I asked her trying to start a pleasant conversation, something we had yet to have.

She looked taken aback for a moment before a smile spread on her lips. "It was amazing."

"How so?" I pressed for more details.

"Well, I enjoyed my job, something I'm sure you can relate to." I smiled at that comment, she wasn't wrong. "And I had friends there."

I wrinkled my brow. "You don't have friends here?"

She thought for a moment. "I guess I do but far fewer and I feel mostly less sincere. They are all worried about what people are wearing and the cars they drive. Not always the most interesting conversations."

I laughed lightly. "Not your cup of tea then? What would you rather talk about?"

"This?" She smiled at me, a smile she hadn't shown me since that first day she came home. It was just as crippling now. I was in trouble here, but I didn't want to stop.

"OK, wait did you get some awfully complicated coffee order and sit around central park drinking it? Pretend you were the main character of the latest rom-com." I teased her.

She laughed, a proper laugh. God it sounded like heaven. "No. I don't really like coffee. I spent most of my time looking for the best place to get a proper cup of tea. And decent chocolate, I nearly went crazy without that." She paused we had broken the tree line, and now stood in the open space in front of the two lakes. "I had grown to love it though, my apartment was lovely and I had such freedom."

"Why did you come back then, surely you could have stayed there?" I wondered briefly if her engagement was the reason.

"Wishing me back to America wouldn't be very nice-ish of you."

"I'm serious it sounds like you had a good thing going over there, did you want to move back?" I wanted to ask about her fiancé.

59

"It was nice but it wasn't home." She looked around the lake. "It hasn't got a patch on this for me."

I nodded in agreement I had always loved the grounds here and now that I lived and worked I don't think I could dream of leaving it for anywhere else. We enjoyed the lake for a while, walking the edge in peaceful silence.

Knowing it might ruin the nice time we were having I finally plucked up the nerve to ask. "When did you get engaged?" I immediately bit my tongue, I wanted to sound like I was just asking a friendly question but even I could tell it sounded harsh. I looked at her expecting to see her angry with me or a little offended at least. She didn't. "Sorry, you don't have to talk about it."

"No it's fine and I'm not sure, is the answer to your question." She fiddled with her reigns not looking at me.

I was confused. "You're not sure?"

Sighing she looked up but still not at me. "If you're going on when he thinks we got engaged then I suppose two weeks. Though I haven't actually been asked." I didn't reply leaving space for her to say what she needed. "I'm not sure I will be either." She stopped before letting out a bitter half-laugh. "Probably because neither he nor my mother would like my answer."

"You don't want to marry him?"

She looked at me amusement playing on her face. "You met him, would you put us together?" She was asking for an outside opinion, but my feelings for her made me very biased. I wouldn't have him breathe the same air as her, never mind marrying her.

"No, it's not the best match I've seen." I chuckled slightly. "Why not just refuse?"

"It's tradition, an arranged marriage to ensure an heir, or profitable business, or whatever." She waved her hand around brushing the words out of the air as she said them.

"I didn't think they would still do that." Irritation threatened my tone, I couldn't believe she would be forced into something like this.

"I was hoping they wouldn't." She agreed. "Anyway, what about you?" I was confused for a moment. "Are you, with anyone?" She looked shy and unsure.

I smiled and contemplated conjuring up some beautiful woman waiting for me at home if only to see her reaction. I chose to be nice-ish. "No, I was a while back but not for some time now." I was worried it came off sad and pathetic but she didn't comment if it did. The smallest of smiles, that she tried to hide, on her lips. She changed the subject after that, asking me about my life in the time she had been away. And the years before that when we didn't see each other.

Too soon we were heading back. I had gotten caught up in how nice today had been. I let my guard down and she had come steaming in, bringing my crush back in full force. It didn't change any facts though, she was engaged and although she didn't like the idea of it, she had made no notion that she planned to get out of it either. The barrier, the distance I had put between her and I had crumbled in a matter of hours.

"That was fun, thank you." She thanked me after we had sorted the horses and re-stabled them. I nodded. "The other day when I said you couldn't come out with Charlie and me. Well if you wanted to again I can't see why not." She was extending an olive branch. Our new friendliness emboldening her to ask me to join them.

"Thank you." I started, "but I won't be joining you. You know Charlie asked me to cover for him. He's your teacher and he's the best we have. I hope I was a decent substitute for you today. If you'll excuse me." I left her standing there bewildered. Self-preservation not allowing me to turn back. I needed to get away from her.

Back in my office, I buried my face in my hands, closing my eyes only brought images of her though. Snapping them open I shook my head trying to make sense of the papers littering my desk. Mike and another lad came in while I was rifling through them, making themselves tea and sitting on the sofa. I read and re-read the same paragraph four times before huffing and throwing it down.

"Uh oh, something stressing you lad?" Mike's voice was joking but I knew he meant the question.

"Mmm." I hummed in response. He had no idea how shot my concentration was.

"I reckon you come for a drink tonight then. Stop working so damn hard." He was firm, and if I knew him as well as I think I did, wouldn't take no for an answer.

"Yeah alright." I resigned knowing I probably needed to take the advice and relax a bit.

"The George it is then, first rounds on you." He raised his mug at me.

8
Luke

By the time we left for 'The George', there was a large group of us. Though most of them were at the age where you never say no to the pub, I'm sure Mike's offer of the first round being on me helped their decisions. The small pub is only a 20-minute walk down into the village, and the evening was nice and warm. This time of year, it stays light until gone 9 pm so the promise of a beer garden spurred us all on through the lanes.

Stepping through the small door, the smell of stale beer and old wood hit me immediately, a strong yet not unpleasant odour. Being Friday night, the pub was already quite busy, though that wasn't saying much, only two dozen people maybe a few less.

"Right, what are we having lads?" I summoned them all to the bar, the barman waiting with his arms on the top as they rattled off the requests. I collected the orders and relayed them back in a less chaotic manner to the older gent. "Four ciders, three lagers and two Guinness please mate." He nodded making the drinks, placing pour after pour on the top. I handed them out to the swarm. "Cheers." I thanked him when he was done, passing him a wad of cash and waiting for my change. I was going to turn and suggest the beer garden when a commotion behind me had the words stopping.

"Charlie!"

"We didn't know you were coming." I saw the lad making his way through the throng to reach the bar. Getting clapped on the shoulder by his mates as he moved.

"Probably heard Luke was paying and wanted a photo!" Some laughter followed.

I raised my pint with one hand and flipped off that last comment with my free one. "What are you drinking?" I asked Charlie who had made it to the bar next to me. I called the barman back over.

"It's OK I'll get it, I'm here with a friend." He declined my offer ordering a couple of drinks himself.

"I don't mind getting his too, come join us we were going to drink outside?" I offered him. He looked unsure.

"Eh I don't know; I'll have to ask her." He tried to make his way back through, but he now had everyone's attention.

"Young Charlie's on a date!"

"Where is she then mate?" A few guys craned their necks around the pub.

He defended. "I'm just having a drink with a friend."

"We've all used that one before!"

"Does this friend have a sister?" Someone joked earning some laughs.

"Leave it out! Don't make the guy more nervous." Charlie looked at me with thanks. "Especially when he's on a date." I watched his face fall as I joined in the teasing.

"It's not a date." He was still trying to iterate.

"OK if it's not a date then come join us?" I persuaded.

"Fine." Charlie was defeated. "Let me just go talk to her." He headed back to his "friend".

We moved away from the bar and to the garden. The lads' laughter died off when they reached the patio, a few of them stopping dead. "Oi watch it!" Mike protested after nearly bumping him and his pint into the back of someone. Moving around them I saw what had caused the standstill. Charlie and his "friend" were in the garden. He stood talking to her, she remained in her seat. He finished what he said, and she looked over at our group. It was Miss Penhall. *Shit, so much for a drink to get my mind off her.*

What was she doing here with him anyway? Are they on a date? She didn't mention it this morning. So many questions played in my mind, irritation creeping from nowhere and leaving a sour taste in my mouth. I watched as she smiled slightly and stood up. Charlie still holding their drinks, lead them over to our group. I could hear a few comments of disbelief, others let out stifled nervous laughs.

"Guys I'm sure you know already, this Natalie." He introduced her, almost unnecessarily, she waved lightly. She looked nervous or guilty. I hadn't decided yet. The guys snapped out of their daze throwing their names at her. She smiled at them. She looked good. Tight blue jeans showing off her legs, she was wearing a large plaid jacket. Relaxed and casual. Maybe it wasn't a date?

I tried to convince myself not to care, it didn't work. She had greeted everyone except myself and Mike. The guys had begun to take up several benches on the lawn.

"Nice to see you Miss." He greeted her with formality.

"Nat, please Mike." She corrected him nicely. He smiled at her.

"No introductions needed here I guess?" Charlie asked rhetorically when he looked at me.

She smiled but it wasn't real. Shaking her head she went to open her mouth but closed it again. I thought to say something but unsure of what I just nodded making my way to a seat. If anyone thought I was rude they didn't say anything. Bad luck for me, I ended up at a table with her, Charlie and Mike also sitting with us.

"Sorry, you have to tell us, how did Charlie manage to get you to go on a date with him?" Tim one of the youngest lads called from the table next to us. I heard Charlie swear under his breath taking a gulp of his cider before glaring at the bloke.

"I told you guys.." He sounded a little pissed off now.

Natalie put a hand to his shoulder stopping him, before looking at Tim. "I'm not on a date with him. We're just friends." I looked at her hand resting on his arm. *Sure.* I wanted to believe her, she sounded sincere. My toxic thoughts wouldn't let me though.
Tim, I think choosing to believe her continued the conversation. "So, are you seeing anyone then?" I chose a poor moment to take a drink nearly laughing it back out at the bold question. He was 19 and still baby-faced. Looking at him, he didn't look embarrassed, maybe the other guys had dared him to do it.

"No, I'm not." Her face still holding the sincerity, but I knew that was a lie. Charlie's eyes flicked to her before going back to his drink. Oh, so he knew of the fiancé too. I couldn't help but wonder what they had spoken about. On their many lessons and here at the pub. Did she tell him everything? Did he listen to all her problems, and soothe her with kindness? I felt the bitter desperation of wishing it was me she confided in. I couldn't do it, I couldn't sit with her as friends, if that was the truth of what was going on here. I wanted so much more from her, with her, so I can have none of it.

I realised I had finished my pint quickly, rising to get another I shook the empty glass at the other tables showing my intention. A few raised empty or near-empty glasses and I nodded heading back inside. Only when he leaned on the top next to me did I know Charlie had followed. I didn't talk to him putting in the order instead. He was the first to speak.

"It's not a date." He stated, not looking at me keeping his eyes on the TV above the bar.

I shrugged. "I don't care who you date Charlie." It sounded bitter to my own ears. He finally dragged his eyes to me, meeting my gaze.

"Didn't say you did boss. Just thought considering who it is you might have wanted to know that it isn't a date. We're just hanging as friends." He nodded at the barman who had placed our drinks down. I paid silently thinking on what he said. I could only come up with the conclusion that he must know how I feel. I couldn't admit it though. Like an addiction, admitting I had a problem would be the first step down a path I was trying hard to avoid.

"What do you mean considering who it is?" I caged my voice.

"Well, just in case you thought it was a conflict of interest. You know she is Lord Penhall's daughter technically all our boss." His reply made sense, but his eyes told me that wasn't the reason for his assurance.

Nodding I grabbed up the drinks, Charlie taking the rest. "OK." I had no more words for him. I think I believed him, but it unsettled me that he knew. What if he told her? I couldn't let that thought idle, pushing it aside as I sat back in my seat. Immediately sinking a few big gulps of cider, I needed my head to not be so clear. I watched as she interacted with Mike and Charlie, everyone having gotten over the initial shock.

"So how was the lesson today?" Charlie looked at both of us. Natalie also looked at me, she still hadn't spoken to me. I wanted her to, but after I rebuffed her earlier, I understood why she didn't. "That bad huh?" Charlie laughed when neither of us responded.

I shook my head. "It was OK."

"Yeah, it was nice...ish," She spoke to Charlie, I smiled into my pint.

"Sorry for not mentioning it was Luke." He didn't look sorry at all. "I guess nice-ish is as much as I could hope for."

"Yeah, I suppose it is." A small smile was on the corner of her lips, I got the feeling it was for me. I warmed at the thought of her thinking about today, thinking about me.

"Where did you go?" He prodded.

"The lakes," I responded now fully invested in the discussion.

"Oh, I have been meaning to take you there." He smiled at her. Beat you to it, pal. Smug pride swelled in my chest.

"They were beautiful," She spoke, wistful in her memory.

"Maybe next lesson we can go there again?" He offered. I scowled wanting her memory to remain mine. Obsessive I know but I couldn't help it.

"Maybe." She didn't sound convinced, and I was pleased. I hoped she wanted it to be our memory too and not that she didn't enjoy it.

Mike headed home not long later; he was on the wake-up shift tomorrow so had to get an early night in. Charlie, tempted by a game of pool from Tim, disappeared inside after Nat insisted he go have fun. "You're the best-est!" He called back and then we were alone.

"So… are you guys celebrating something?" She nodded at the group, speaking to me for the first time this evening. I must have looked taken aback because she added. "What?"

"I'm surprised you're talking to me. And no we aren't." I answered both questions keeping my voice flat.

Scowling in response. "I didn't think you would want to talk to me. You don't usually."

"Right," I replied sarcastically.

"Am I wrong?" She challenged.

"Yes," I replied coolly. "I talked to you today, thought you said you had a nice time?"

"Nice-ish." She corrected. "You made it very clear that you only did that as a favour to Charlie."

71

"Think what you want Natalie." I knew I was being petty.

"Think what I..." She stuttered. "It's hardly thinking what I want when I'm going off what you tell me." She was whisper shouting. The other tables now mostly empty and no one listening or caring for our conversation. "Am I supposed to just guess when you're lying?"

"You're one to talk of lies." I chided back.

"What are you talking about?" She looked genuinely curious.

"You're not on a date with Charlie?" I knew they probably weren't, but I needed her to confirm it to my face.

"We are friends, I know friendship and kindness is a concept you struggle with, but you can *just* be friends with someone of the opposite gender."

I agreed except when it came to her, we were never going to be just friends. "And you're not seeing anyone?" I ignored her jibe and instead called her out on another lie.

"I'm not seeing anyone."

"No, I suppose when you're engaged it doesn't count as dating any more does it?" She looked around, nerves on her face. "Keeping that one between us then? And your best bud?" It was wrong to tease her, but the bitterness wouldn't let me stop.

"You're a prick, Luke Taylor." She stood up leaving without another word. I didn't follow her. I should have. I know I overstepped. Charlie came out of the pub moments later, making his way straight to me.

"What did you do?" He accused. "Nat looks royally pissed."

"No offence Charlie, you are the last person I want to talk to right now." I stood choosing to go home, very much not in the mood to drink or socialise anymore.

I arrived at work the next morning feeling worse for wear. Not because I drank too much, although I probably had a few more than I meant to. Mostly because of how I behaved towards Nat, I was starting to think that my pushing her away was just making me into an asshole.

I resigned myself to mucking out stalls, trying to sweat last night off. I hadn't been at it long when I heard voices out in the walkway. I didn't immediately recognise either of them. I was about to leave the stall to see who it was when their conversation had me pausing to eavesdrop instead.

"Has she warmed up to the idea yet?"

"I don't think so the breakfast we had was dreadful." I creased my brow, that voice I recognised slightly but couldn't place.

"Well, do you think she will marry you then?" It clicked then where I had heard the voice before. Natalie's fiancé, the other guy must be a friend of his.

"She doesn't have a choice." Some nasty laughter followed. I bit my tongue.

"Yeah, but if she doesn't want to marry you will you want to marry her?"

"Of course, you saw the manor. And the title. Mate, I'd be a Lord." He bragged to the unnamed man. "She's pretty easy on the eyes too, it's not like she's ugly. So, there's that." I could feel my anger rising.

"Yeah, but if she doesn't like you what good is it? You haven't got a chance in hell she will let you near her." His friend mocked.

Scoffing. "I'm not going to give her a choice."

"Yeah OK." His friend didn't believe his threat.

"I'm serious, it's her job to produce me an heir. She will do it; I'll tie her down if I have to." I had heard enough. Stepping out of the stall the two men had their back to me a little way further down.

"You should try to be more respectful." I was seething but kept a distance between us. I wouldn't help anyone by knocking him out.

They turned, obviously startled to find they weren't alone. The friend, a weasel of a man looked scared until he saw that his friend was unfazed by my presence. "Why?" He had crossed his arms and was looking at me the same way he did the morning we met.

"Hate for someone to let slip what was just said. I doubt Lord Penhall would appreciate it." I shrugged my shoulders.

"Are you threatening me?" He stepped closer. His anger issues clear on his face.

I smirked.

That irritated him more, he advanced closing the gap step after step. His friend put an arm on his shoulder stopping his attack. "Do you know who this is?" He was asking me. I dragged my eyes to him shaking my head.

"Nah." I did, well I knew who he was to Natalie but other than that.

"This is Mr Layton the future Lord of this estate, your boss."

I looked him up and down. "Mr Layton, was it? I don't see it myself." I made the final step to him; aware he was now in swinging distance. I smiled. "Any man that speaks of someone like that let alone his wife isn't much of a man, never mind a Lord." I curled my lip in disgust. "And certainly not anyone I would have as my boss."

He smiled at me; it was all venom. "Good, then you're fired."

I laughed loudly and genuinely. "You can't fire me." I could see him trying to fumble a sentence together. "Here's what you can do. You can apologise for what you said about Natalie, you can then stay the hell away from her. And for good measure, you could also fuck off? How does that sound?" He shoved me hard in the chest, I stumbled back slightly but I saw it coming so it didn't catch me off guard. I just laughed at him more. "I'm already pretty pissed off today mate, I'd hate to mess up whatever it is you have going on with your hair." I wanted him to attack me. Give me more of an excuse. I held my arms out very much in a come-get-me way. I think it's a good deal."

"You fucking scum!" He screamed at me trying to land a punch, but I was out of his reach, dodging it easily.

I was all smiles, watching this clown embarrass himself. "Come on now, you can do better than that!" I was about to swing back.

"What on earth is going on here?" A loud voice caught us all off guard. Lord Penhall stood some meters away down the hallway. I looked between him and Mr Layton, this would be interesting.

As he approached Mr Layton held his hand up in an accusatory point in my direction. "Him. I want him fired. He threatened me and when I dismissed him, he attacked me." I rolled my eyes. Lord Penhall looked at me, I held my hands up showing I didn't know what he was on about.

"My office now." The Lord spoke with no room for further argument, I nodded my head. Mr Layton smiled victoriously. "Both of you." That wiped the look off of his face. The three of us made our way from the stables.

9
Natalie

Last night had been fun, outside of Luke's tantrum that is. Before they had all arrived Charlie and I had gotten to talk. I told him about my engagement. He was understandably shocked and if anything, a little angry. I think of my being forced into something I didn't want. And after a brief description of Peter, I don't think he blamed me for my hesitancy. I had stayed later than I thought I would. Drinking and even playing some pool with a few of the guys. It had felt so normal and easy, Charlie had been right it was what I needed.

My phone rang, Charlie.

"Good morning." I sing-songed down the phone to him.

"Natalie." He didn't sound very happy, and I sat up straighter on my sofa at his tone. "Mr Layton fired Luke."

I froze. "W…what?" Panic passed through me. I'm not sure why but my stomach knotted in worry, and I spoke frantically to Charlie. "He can't do that surely. What happened?"

"No one knows, they had a fight in the stables and then Mr Layton fired him and now they're with your dad." He spewed the information.

"I have to go." I hung up rushing from my room. Why were they fighting? How could my father let Peter fire Luke? And why did it bother me so much? I took the stairs two at a time, my frustration and worry building with every step. I stormed into my father's office, not bothering with knocking. I marched up to his desk ranting as I went.

"Mr Layton cannot fire Luke he has no authority to! Luke hasn't done anything wrong and shouldn't be thrown out after all the years his family have put into this place!" I was breathing deeply but my father appeared calm. No sign of my outburst having angered him, his fingers steepled together on his desk. He looked at the two chairs in front of him, as did I. They were occupied. Both Luke and Mr Layton were staring at me like I'd grown two heads, though Peter also looked incredibly angry. I looked between them growing more embarrassed by the second when Lord Penhall cleared his throat.

"I had just finished explaining to Mr Layton that he exactly does not hold the authority to fire my staff. I also reassured *Mr Taylor* that his position here is secure." He emphasised 'Mr Taylor' whilst looking at me. Oh, so he was angry. "Gentlemen, if you would excuse us." My father rose from his seat and the two men followed suit.

I waited for the others to leave. Mr Layton made sure to give me a scathing glare as he left, Luke refused to meet my eye, as they left me to my fate. Gesturing to the seat in front of him I sat and waited for the telling off.

"Natalie you know better than to enter my office without knocking." I stared at my fingers feeling like a little girl. "I appreciate your passion on these kinds of matters, the estate after all will be yours one day. Not Mr Layton's. Do you understand what I'm saying?"

My eyes widened. "Does that mean..."

"No, it doesn't mean I'm calling off your engagement, it means you inherit this estate, not him. It will always be yours; it is your birth right. But that does mean that you will feel more strongly about things than he will. I only ask that you are patient with Mr Layton, he will make foolish mistakes, but I need to know that you can take responsibility. Outbursts like this are not professional nor are they helpful." He paused his eyes pleading with mine.

"Now onto the matter of your manners lately. While it's nice to see you getting passionate over the people that work for us and the estate goings on, please address Mr Taylor as such. This first name basis you've got is too familiar. Does he call you Natalie?"

"No, he calls me Miss Penhall."

"Good the man has manners, see that you take his example. You may go."

I left his office feeling an odd mix of emotions, I was glad Luke wasn't fired, but still not quite sure why it bothered me so much that he might have been. He had been nothing but a thorn in my side the entire time I had been home. And my father's lecture was nothing like I was expecting. On one hand, I was glad to be reassured of my position in this arrangement, on the other he still had firm faith in my union with Mr Layton.

I'd always used Maria's first name and it had never been an issue. My father unlike my mother was not so prideful to assume we couldn't address others by their first names. I remember him calling Luke's dad Charles instead of Mr Taylor on several occasions. I'd imagine he also calls Luke by his name, so why set rules when it comes to me? I turned the corner still lost in thought and bumped straight into a hard chest. Stumbling back slightly I looked up at the obstacle. Peter.

"Mr Layton." I curtly addressed him while trying to sidestep around. He matched my movement blocking my path again.

"You can call me Peter you know." He smiled at me, a sickening mocking to the expression.

"I think it more appropriate for me to address you as Mr Layton." This time I successfully managed to skirt around him.

"You must be very close with Mr Taylor to address him by his first name then when you won't do the same for your fiancé." His words had me pausing and turning to look back at him. Why was everyone so hung up on that? I held up my left hand and brought it close to my face inspecting it thoroughly.

"Odd I would have thought if I was engaged this is exactly where a ring would be." I threw an exaggerated puzzled look into the mix.

"Soon enough there will be," He stated with irritation.

"Don't hold your breath." I smiled sweetly at him and continued on my way.

I went straight to the stables looking for Mr Taylor. I looked around the barn and couldn't see him, and he hadn't been in the paddocks out front. Making my way to the tack room I peeked into several of the stalls to see if he was mucking any of them out. I opened the tack room door to find it empty, stepping inside I breathed in the leather and wood smell. I ran my hand over a saddle that was on the workbench.

"Can I help you Miss?" I jumped a mile and glared at Luke who had now appeared at the tack room door. He didn't look pleased to see me.

"I just wanted to check that you were OK I guess and apologise for Mr Layton's behaviour."
He nodded never breaking eye contact his hand gripping a pair of reigns. "Why did he try to fire you?"

He thought something over for a moment. "You should ask your fiancé."

I gritted my teeth. "Yeah, like he would tell me."

"Well, then you shouldn't worry about it."

"Well of course I'm going to worry about it!"

He stepped further into the room. "It doesn't matter it's sorted."

"Of course it matters, he tried to get you sacked!"

"But I wasn't so it's all fine."

"Why won't you tell me?" My voice had grown louder. I was beginning to get irritated with the secrecy.

"Fine, we got into an argument, and I might have threatened him. Just a bit though." He still wouldn't look at me. I knew I was only getting half the story.

"And the argument was abouttt....?" I drew the word out hoping to coax the rest out of him.

He sighed sounding exhausted. "You...mostly."

"Me?" I furrowed my brow puzzled as to why they would argue over me. "Why?"

"Because that pig you are marrying was spouting some rubbish to his friend. Making horrible comments about you." He paused breathing heavily "About what he was going to do to you on your wedding night. How he'd make you see how much of a man he was. Because I stood up for you, he tried to fire me." Luke looked furious, he threw the reigns onto a nearby bench making me start.

I suddenly felt very small all the fight and irritation leaving me. Fear gnawed at the edge of my chest, confusion following through flooding my thoughts. "But you don't even like me, why would you risk your job like that."

He ran a hand down his face stepping further into the room. Looking up to the ceiling considering something. When he brought his eyes back down to me all anger was gone from them he studied my face. "He fired me because he could clearly see something you can't. That I do like you. He doesn't like that I like you."

My breath felt constricted. No no, he did not like me. "You like me? But you barely talk to me. And when you do it's mostly mean or at best antagonistic. You even told me the first day I was back that you didn't like me."

"I lied. To keep you away. I can't, I shouldn't feel this way about you." He looked at the confusion still evident on my features. "You are infuriating, I can't stop thinking about you and you just waltz around completely oblivious to what you're doing to me. Because I can't have you. Because this can't ever happen" He gestured between us.

He stopped, looking at me with real pain in his eyes. He had left me completely dumbfounded, finally looking away. He rubbed the back of his neck "Uh, if you could just forget..."

"Who said I don't like you?" My voice was quiet and low, if his head hadn't snapped in my direction, I'd have thought I didn't say it aloud.

"What did you say?"

I replied with more confidence and volume. "You never asked. Maybe I like you."

"Don't do that."

"What?"

"Humour me."

"I'm not. I do like you when you aren't being an arse that is."

"You can't like me Natalie."

"I can and I do. So, what are you going to do about it?"

He walked steadily towards me until we were almost nose to nose. His eyes searched mine for any lie, glancing down at my lips.

"Fuck it" The words sighed out of his lips before he crashed them into mine. I grasped his shoulders to stop myself from falling off balance. He wrapped his arms around me pulling me ever closer. Our kisses were wet, heavy, desperate. I relaxed my hands running them up his neck and into his soft hair. He backed us up to the wall until I was pressed flush between the wood and him. His hand propped by my head the other caressing my jaw. I realised how much I needed this, how much I needed him. Heat flooded through me, and I could feel how much he wanted me. His tongue explored my mouth, dragging soft moans from me. I let him dominate our kiss and my mind.

I heard a noise from the stable. Peter, someone was with him. I pushed Luke away slightly, listening out. He pulled his head back listening and catching his breath.

"You should have seen her all worked up and fiery over him. I don't know how her dad didn't see it. She was practically feral."

"So why didn't he get fired?" The second person spoke.

"Because Lord Penhall has a soft spot for the runt." I glanced at Luke who still hovered over me looking towards the door. Many words could describe him, but runt was definitely not one of them.

"What are you gonna do then? She clearly also has a soft spot for him." His friend was goading him on.

"Don't worry I'm still going to marry the stuck-up cow, then we will see how feral she can really get." They both laughed. Luke stiffened and went to move to the door; I placed a hand on his arm stopping him. Shaking my head silently pleading that he'd leave it. "I'll see him fired and well away from what belongs to me just you wait."

The voices receded further into the stable and I turned my eyes to Luke. His were closed and the hand that was resting on my waist was gripping it as if to keep himself tethered to me. "Please let me kill him?" He whispered and I couldn't tell if he was asking me or himself.

"Luke." his eyes opened at my voice, softening as they looked at me. I would be the end of him if we did this. He couldn't fight Peter every time I wasn't here to stop him. This was a mistake. "I should go, we shouldn't have done this." I looked at him but he remained leaning on the wall. I went to leave assuming he wouldn't be saying anything. I removed his hand and slipped out from underneath him.

"Do you care that much if your fiancé knows? Why does his opinion of you matter so much he evidently doesn't have a very high one already." He had turned and was spitting the words out, bitterness lacing through them. I knew he was angry and that the hate wasn't aimed at me but today was still my fault.

"His opinion of me doesn't matter in the slightest."

"Then why?" He asked taking a step towards me.

I held my hand up stopping him in his tracks. "I won't be the reason you lose your job. Everything you have worked so hard for."

"That's my choice to make."

I shook my head showing I thought he was wrong. "No, it's not. It's mine. I won't let your unhappiness be my fault." I turned to leave again.

"If you walk away then my unhappiness is inevitable Natalie." I had stopped and I think it gave him hope. "You

87

think now I know how you feel I'll be able to stay away?"

I sighed my hand on the back door handle " I hope so, for your sake." Then I left as the tears spilled from my eyes.

10
Luke

I had gotten no work done. 11 Am on a Monday and I had done nothing but sit in my office and think of Natalie. I had kissed her. Told her how I felt, and confirmed feelings I wasn't sure of right up until I was confessing them to her. She rejected me. I frowned to myself. She kissed me back; told me she wanted me and then that prick. My fists clenched thinking of Mr Layton. But hadn't she defended him, or was she just protecting me?

I thought about her storming into Lord Penhall's office. All fire and fury trying to save me from the chopping block. I had been dumbstruck, to be honest, I half expected her to back up Mr Layton. If anyone should want me dismissed it would be her. I had more than deserved it after how I had treated her. I truly didn't know how I would stay away now we had kissed. I wanted her more now than ever. My mind tried to think of any way and every way we could be together. Any opportunity for me to see her again.

My head was still swimming when Charlie came into the office. He nodded in my direction before going to the kettle. We hadn't exactly been on speaking terms since Friday night. He was very close to Natalie, and I could see how it would help me. Maybe he could get her to talk to me or listen to me at least.

"Charlie, a word." I motioned to the seat in front of me. He walked over sitting without replying. "I wanted to apologise for Friday night. I had had a few too many and well I'm sorry."

He nodded. "Thanks." Stopping to think he continued. "You might punch me for this." I raised a brow now curious. "But if I saw someone out with the girl I liked I'd probably have acted the same if not worse so I can understand."

"I don't…"

"Sure you don't," He smirked.

Sighing I resigned to having to confide in him. "How long have you known?"

"Since the day of her first lesson. It was very obvious that you both had it bad."

"Both?"

"Yeah, there's no way you get under someone's skin like that unless you let them, she might not know it but she's into you."

Oh, I think she knows it, I thought to myself, but knowing about it and doing something about it are very different things.

"And you two are friends?"

He rolled his eyes at me "Yes friends. Same as I told you Friday night."

"She won't talk to me." I stated. I hated it but I needed to ask him for help.

"I wonder why." He drawled though I couldn't help but think that for his sarcasm he didn't know the real reason. And it was much worse than a drunken blunder.

"Yeah, well I need to talk to her. So I was hoping I could crash your next lesson?"

Charlie drew his brow together looking somewhere between concerned and disheartened. "She cancelled."

"Oh." I paused, "well maybe Friday?"

He shook his head. "No, she cancelled all week and gave me a vague answer about next week." He stood and grabbed his tea. "I'm not saying it's because of you but if there is even a chance it is, I hope you can fix it. The lessons were good for her."

I nodded as he left.

I would find a way to see her.

11

Natalie

The days rolled away from me and before I knew it, a week had passed since that day in the stables. I hadn't been near them since. Mostly so that I didn't have to look at Luke, see the disappointment and hurt. Damage I had done. I also knew that I still felt the same way about him. All the rationalising and pragmatic thinking I could conjure had done nothing to stop my desire for him. A small part of me knew that I wouldn't or couldn't resist him if I found myself alone with him again. But, I couldn't be so cruel to him, this could never happen and to drag him down because of my selfishness would be so wrong. He was a good man who deserved more than to end up tangled in my drama.

A soft tap on my bedroom door had me uncurling from my spot on the sofa. Putting the book I hadn't really been reading down I smoothed my clothes and called out. "Come in."

Maria entered the room her warm eyes finding mine. "The guests will be arriving soon, your mother requests you in the garden to welcome them."

I nodded making my way to the mirror on the wall. "Thank you, Maria, I'll be down in a moment." I replied looking at her. Maria smiled, looking like she wanted to say something extra but thought better of it, leaving me staring at my reflection. My hair would need sorting before I went down, small sections had broken free of my low ponytail. I went to the dresser in my wardrobe to redo the style, adding a few more pins to combat any summer breeze. I assessed the rest of my outfit, thankful that my moping had not creased my sundress and I wouldn't have to change. I grabbed some sandals to pair with the calf-length garment before heading out to join my mother and father.

Today was important to my mother, lots of their friends were coming and a couple of girlfriends I had had before leaving would also be here. I plastered a big smile on my face before stepping out onto the patio. Today would be hard work. It's not that I didn't particularly like any of the guests and in the case of my friends, it would be nice to catch up with them. It was more the event as a whole that was daunting, my parents hosted this garden party every year, including the years I was gone. This year I was home, and supposedly proudly engaged, my mother would have been waiting for this moment. She was going to show-boat and boast shamelessly all day, for me that meant a very uncomfortable afternoon of having to answer questions. And an afternoon of having one Peter Layton draped over me. After hearing his thoughts on me the other day and coupled with what Luke had told me, the idea of spending any time with him filled me with dread.

Already two guests had arrived, and I made my way over to my parents who were already deep in conversation with them. "And here she is!" My mother beamed pulling me closer. "I was just telling Mr and Mrs Milligan how excited you are for your upcoming nuptials!" Her squeeze on my hand was sharp and enough of a warning to elicit some feigned enthusiasm from me.

"I am, every little girl dreams of her wedding day, but with it so close now. It's almost overwhelming." I spoke carefully, flashing the ageing couple a hopefully sincere smile.

Mrs Milligan gushed placing a hand over her chest, clutching imaginary pearls I guessed. "And your dashing husband to be Mr Layton is a perfect gentleman, you're a very lucky young lady." I bit the inside of my cheek to stop from saying something I'd regret. The most perfectly timed glass of lemonade was offered to me by a server. I took a thankful sip, freeing myself from any further conversation for the moment. This type of conversation would be the theme of the day, my only hope was to get through it without revealing too much of my disdain for Peter.

Peter arrived a couple of hours into the festivities, up until then I had avoided most of the detailed questions. My friends Lisa and Hettie had arrived an hour prior and after the initial Q&A, I had steered the conversation towards more general topics. They had both gotten married since I had been away, I'd sent gifts. Accompanied by their husbands today but, as with most functions in this world, the children had been left at home with their nannies I was glad of that. Not that I don't like children, it was just one less avenue of questioning I was happy to avoid. The thought of reproducing with my fiancé nearly had me bringing back up my drink.

Peter, and his ever-faithful sidekick Liam, strutted down the lawn through the spattering of party-goers. The image of charm shaking hands as he went, greeting the women with a small bow and kiss of the hand. I curled my lip watching the scene, class A actor this one. If I didn't know any better, I would also be amongst those congratulating his fiancée.

"Who's that?" I followed Lisa's gaze my own eyes landing on who had gotten her attention. Luke was walking down the path towards the stable.

"That's just the grounds manager." I hoped I sounded dismissive, praying that the nerves tumbling around my stomach didn't falter my voice. All three of us were still staring at him when he looked up. I faintly heard the two ladies beside me giggle like a pair of schoolgirls caught misbehaving. He looked at me for only a moment before averting his eyes and carrying on down the path. But it was long enough. The fog of sadness and pity for myself had nudged into the corners of my mind the second our eyes connected. His expression was closed, unreadable, indifferent. I probably looked on the verge of tears. It's what I had told him to do wasn't it, so why did it hurt so much?

"What a beautiful distraction that must be." Lisa's girlish voice came from behind me. I pushed down the tears and turned to clap back at the perverted remark. I didn't get a chance to however as a hand curled around my waist.

"What's a beautiful distraction?" Peters' sickly smooth voice asked. He glanced between all three of us raising a perfectly groomed brow. Hettie and Lisa looked between each other before looking back down the garden to where Luke had just approached the stables.

"Nothing."

"Just enjoying the scenery." They both chimed feigning innocence. Peter stiffened next to me, only momentarily dropping the charming smile to glare at Luke's retreating frame.

"I'm sure we can find you ladies a better view." His voice was light and flirtatious, his tone eliciting more giggles from the pair. His fingers betrayed his true feeling as they dug viscously into my hip, punishing me for my friend's leering. I bit the inside of my cheek to stop from crying out.

"Hmmm I'm not sure, I mean the view is pretty good from what I can see." Lisa continued to tease all the while glancing in the direction of the stables. She had always been the flirty type, only now her flirtations were getting me in trouble instead of herself. I was surely going to have a mark where Peter's grip was still firm on my side, and I felt tears well behind my eyes. These were angry though, angry at Peter, angry at my parents and angry at myself. Only after I shifted uncomfortably did he stop. His hand remained in place now laid over the sore area, but at least he had stopped digging his nails in.

I stood mute at his side after that, nodding when I felt a topic needed my input. Trying to keep my mouth shut, certain that if I were to open it the only thing that would come out would be a sob.

"So, Natalie, when is he going to officially ask you?" Hettie's question caught me off guard and I looked at her expectant expression with a blank one of my own. I had only half been paying attention, last I tuned in they were discussing Polo, but that didn't fit the question.

"Huh?" I dumbly asked deciding not to grasp at the straws of half-heard topics. She rolled her eyes in return smiling. Waggling her left hand at me, hers sporting a giant diamond bridal set.

"It's not official until you get the ring sweetie!" She winked teasing me. I smiled back because I knew how it looked without a ring on my finger, and I was in no rush to change that.

"I know." I absent-mindedly looked at my left hand even adding a sigh for effect. "But there's no rush is there? Besides I don't mind waiting." I shrugged sweetly at the woman. Peter and I were the only ones present who knew how true that was.

"Oh." She seemed taken aback by my nonchalance but quickly recovered. "Well, when were you thinking for the ceremony, if you don't act soon," She glanced at Peter, "you'll be getting married at Christmas!" She giggled, and Lisa interjected gushing about a Christmas wedding and how they 'haven't had a good wedding in ages.' I spoke over both of them.

"No, I don't think I want a winter wedding. I think May is the perfect month or maybe early June." I creased my brow as though giving it serious thought, though all I had done was pick the date furthest from now.

"Next year?!" The shock was evident. People in our world didn't usually have such long engagements. I mean when you had the money and means to throw together a wedding at the drop of a hat, why bother? And when most marriages were for the sake of profit or social gain, people didn't tend to dally.

"As I said, there's no real rush." I took a delicate sip of my glass hiding the smirk at their reactions. I didn't bother looking at Peter I knew he would be angry. Outside of the group, I noticed my father disappearing into the house. "If you'll excuse me, I have to speak with my father." I shuffled free from Peter heading in the direction of Lord Penhall. Glad to be away from the tension I stepped into the cool kitchen taking a few steadying breaths.

Lord Penhall who had been at the sink when I entered turned to greet me. "Natalie, are you having fun?" The real answer was of course no, and the thought of my bruised hip popped into my head. I'd have to check that in a moment, for now, I needed my father in an agreeable mood.

"I am thank you." I stood further into the room. Picking up a glass of lemonade from a serving tray, I took a sip looking at the back of my father's head. "I actually wanted to ask you something."

"Oh?" The back of his head responded.

"Would I be able to join you tomorrow?" A few seconds passed. "At the agricultural show." I clarified my question still waiting for a reply.

"Why?" He was looking at me now. The question wasn't mean or dismissive. He just sounded curious.

"I've been thinking about what you said and you're right. The manor will be my responsibility so I should probably learn from you where I can." He released a breath through his nose and seemed to be considering my request.

"Your mother mentioned needing you for something tomorrow, we will find some other way for you to learn." My heart sank with disappointment, but I knew better than to fight him on this. Agreeing to help me some other way was still a win. I turned to go back to the party just as my mother walked into the kitchen.

"Why are you two hiding out in here?" She glanced between us. "Natalie, Peter will be looking for you, this is a good opportunity for you to mingle as a couple."

"Relax my dear, Natalie was just asking if she could join me tomorrow." Lady Penhall opened her mouth to protest but my father didn't leave room. "I told her you had plans for the two of you." He passed her and headed outside.

"Oh yes, we do have plans." She enthused and grasped my hands in hers. "We…" cue dramatic pause "are wedding planning tomorrow!" Squeezing my captured fingers Mother beamed at me. My heart sunk further, anything but that.

"I hardly see the need to plan a wedding that I don't intend on being at." I bit out.

She sighed. "Don't ruin today Natalie."

"But Mr Layton…" I fully intended to tell her and even show her what I'm sure would be a mark on my side. She held up her hand stopping me.

"I won't hear it anymore. He has been nothing but gentile to you and you keep trying to sting him." She scolded me.

She turned on her heel still grasping my hands and pulled me in the direction of the patio doors.

"Just a moment." I released from her grip, causing her to pause in step and look at me, stern concern in her eyes. "I need to use the bathroom." She relaxed waving me off.

"Oh of course see you out there!" She trilled over her shoulder. Rolling my eyes, I set off for my bedroom. Once there I went straight to my bathroom locking the door behind me. Standing in front of the mirror I pulled up my sundress to reveal my hip. Peter's mark of anger was already purpling. Four red bites from his fingernails glared from the centre of the mark. Dampening a towel with some cold water I pressed it to my skin hoping to subdue the painful sting. I hissed at the contact. Drying myself off I gently pulled my dress back down trying not to brush it against my hip too much. Any pity I had held for myself, and my situation had long since dispersed and I was left with renewed determination. I was not marrying that pig.

His true colours are as clear as that bruise and I had no doubts that was just the beginning of his dark side. There was no doubt in my mind that what he had said in the barn the other day was more than just jovial banter. They were threats I was sure he would carry out given half the chance. I would find a way out of this but for now, I must play house. Pretend all is well so no one suspects. I fixed my makeup a little and went back to the party. The day was nearly over, and people would be leaving soon, I could bite my tongue for just a while longer.

I poured some milk into my tea as my mother placed yet another binder onto the kitchen island. Six binders. Six innocent-looking ivory binders. The contents of which made my stomach turn in knots.

"Right, I've picked some themes and colour schemes. I put each into its own binder so we can thoroughly look at them and choose one." My mother had a beaming smile, her hands smoothing the surface of each binder like a prized show dog. Her happiness only faltered when she looked up at me. I was looking at each ivory devil like it might snap open and bite me.

"You've chosen?" My mother's smile fell even more. "Am I to have no say in this?" I queried more to my cup than to her. However, this was the wrong thing to say. When I looked back up the smile was back with renewed enthusiasm.

"No Natalie, not at all, if you have a theme or colour in mind." She was rambling animatedly pulling a colour palette from a nearby binder. "We can look at as many as you want, it has to be perfect, after all, you only get one wedding!" Or none at all I thought sarcastically. I mentally slapped myself, my mother, due to my error now thought the only issue I had with marrying Peter was the colour of my bridesmaid dresses. I went to open my mouth, to somehow get some damage control on the situation, but we were both interrupted.

My father knocked on the frame of the open door before walking towards us. Lady Penhall greeted him enthusiastically. "Oh, my love we are having a great time, Natalie was just going to start perusing her options." If only that were true mother, my options looked very different to hers. Hers involved chapels and bouquets, mine were more geared towards tack rooms and the smell of leather. Before I could get carried away by that particular memory my mother's shrill tones bought me back to the room looking at her now pouting at my father.

"But why, you know I planned to do this today. Do you have any idea how long it took to make all those binders?" I tried not to roll my eyes, knowing full well they would have been dictated to my mother's assistant, who actually then made the binders.

"My dear the agricultural show isn't on all year. You have plenty of time for this later." My father's tone was gentle but left no room for discussion.

"I'm sorry what's going on?" I asked having snapped back to the room halfway through their exchange.

"Your father," My mother began pointedly looking at him "has decided he requires your presence today." I jumped up from my chair so quickly I nearly upset my now empty cup.

"Really? I thought you said it wasn't necessary for me to go?" even as I spoke, I wondered why I was questioning this last-minute salvation.

"I changed my mind; it would be good for you to see how things are done. It'll be your responsibility to go someday." I beamed at him and made my way to the door.

"Oh Natalie, wouldn't you rather stay and try to get some wedding things sorted?" My mother asked her voice disappointed and pleading.

"I really would like to go with Father today. I'm sure the options you picked are lovely." I squeezed her hand; despite this arranged marriage disagreement I didn't want to upset her. We didn't do much together so it would have been lovely to spend the day with her, under different circumstances. I released her hand and grabbed my coat from the rack, quickly swapping my shoes for a pair of boots. "Plus, Mr Layton has yet to formally propose, so we have plenty of time anyway." A frown creased her brow at my words.

"That is just a formality Natalie, you are his Fiancée. A proposal isn't necessary." She had turned back into her strict proper self, all signs of mother-daughter bonding gone. I fastened the buttons on my coat.

"Well, it's necessary to me." Father and I left her standing forlorn in the hallway, only a hint of guilt on my mind.

12
Natalie

I followed my father to his car, and he climbed up behind the wheel of his old green range rover. I stepped up into the passenger seat buckling my seatbelt I glanced out the back window. "Are we going alone?" I enquired. There wasn't a livestock box attached to the car, but I had seen no other vehicle or grounds workers around.

"Hmm? Oh, they're meeting us there." My father seemed lost in thought for a moment before pulling out onto the driveway. We remained silent for a while, and I took the time to relax into the seat and the scenery. The change from how I thought this day was going to go, to now, was unexpected and frankly fantastic. I hadn't felt this at ease since I had got back home, I was reminded of the days I would ride out to the farm every week with my father.

"Do you know the last time we drove together like this? I think you were no more than ten years old." Next to me, my father voiced my thoughts aloud. I smiled over at him, looking at his profile as he drove, seeing if I could remember him when I was that age. His hair wasn't so grey back then, and although no great achievement, he used to smile more. He was always stern, yes, but on the car rides out to the farm he would try to relax, for me.

"I was just remembering the same thing."

"And then you became a teenager, a young lady. Always running off with your friends. Giggling over boys." I looked at my hands feeling guilty for discarding my father's company so easily though I hadn't realised it at the time. "Ah, you got busy." He waved it off.

"I could say the same for you." I quipped back but both of us were smiling content in our teasing. We spent the rest of the drive in pleasant conversation, it wasn't long before we were parking up in one of the designated fields. It may have seemed silly to some, but I was incredibly excited for the day, I hadn't been to the show since I was very small. My father came only for business and my mother had taken me along once. She vowed never again. It was both her and my first and only time. Mother hadn't been enamoured with the muddy fields and seemingly endless marquees filled with various animals and their accompanying smells.

Trudging across the field I was glad to have changed footwear, though it hadn't rained the ground was pretty chewed up from the constant traffic of people, animals and vehicles. We entered the first tent; it had been turned into a sort of welcome room and information area. My father excused himself and headed to one of the folding tables that lined the sides. I shuffled myself away from the entrance and the flow of people, perusing the posters that were tacked to the tent wall. There was so much going on over the weekend. Different shows and events. A sheepdog exhibition would be held tomorrow, a shame really as we were only here for the day and would miss it. I was certain there would be plenty to do today if the crowds were anything to go by.

"Miss Penhall." A voice addressed me from behind making me start slightly. I turned coming face to face with Luke and several of the farmhands who had come along to help out. I smiled lightly trying to hide some of the other emotions stirring in me. He looked good in his check shirt and jeans, like an effortlessly handsome cowboy, minus the hat.

"Mr Taylor." I kept my tone even, Father joining us almost as the words left my mouth.

"Ah Mr Taylor, chaps, are we ready to head on?" Lord Penhall addressed the group nodding at Luke and the others. He handed a folded paper itinerary to Luke and one to me. I looked over the paper noting the small marks my father had made next to certain events and stalls. I flipped the paper over viewing the handy map on the back. The whole thing had been set up over four fields so this would come in handy. "If you boys head over to field two that's where they seem to have put the trade stalls, see if you can find the items we discussed there. Oh, and if you see anything else of interest or use call me so I can come and check it out, thank you." The group of men nodded at my father and headed off I presume in the direction of field two. Luke stayed with us.

"Shall we?" My father gestured forward with his hand. I nodded and the three of us headed out the other side of the tent. Luke walked a step or two behind us, his presence

107

making me nervous and awkwardly fumbling for something to break the tension. Even if I was the only one who felt it.

"Can I ask you something?" I finally spoke looking at my father as we walked.

"Of course." He replied, "Today is a learning experience for you, ask away."

"You send the others off to look at the trade stock, wouldn't you rather go yourself?"

"I trust them to make the right decisions and choices on my behalf, plus I'll be too busy looking at the livestock."

"So would you trust them to also look at the livestock?" I didn't want to annoy with persistent questions, but I desperately wanted to learn, to prove I could run the estate on my own.

"No, I would, especially with Mr Taylor here for guidance." He gestured to Luke walking behind us, who remained quiet.

"Then and forgive me if this is a silly question, why do you bother coming along at all?"

"Not a silly question, but one with several answers. Firstly, it's good business to be interested in your business. It's easy to become unconcerned with the goings on of the estate when you disconnect too much from it." I nodded in understanding. "Also, a lot of people I do business with and trade with use the show, seeing me here physically handling things gives a better impression leading to better deals. And lastly, because I enjoy it." This last statement shocked me a little and I looked at my father who now had a small smile on his face. "It gets me outside away from the paperwork and my phone. It's a part of my work that doesn't feel so much like work."

We entered a tent in the next field filled with chickens for sale and show, all displayed in their cages with breed labels attached. We had always kept chickens on the estate, but I had no idea there were this many breeds. The noise of clucking was almost overwhelming, you couldn't hear much past the person next to you.

"Penhall!" A loud voice from the edge of the tent called out. My father turned to the voice then back to Luke and me ushering us to continue while he goes over to the man who caught his attention. I was now alone with Mr Taylor, the first time since we shared that kiss. Though I had no doubt a repeat was likely in the middle of 200 chickens my heart still sped up. With no small talk to fill the space, we walked quietly down the first row of cages.

"Are you enjoying your day?" Luke's voice came from beside me, low but still just audible over the endless clucking.

"I am, thank you, immensely more than the alternative." I pulled a face and turned to look at the cage in front of me.

"I thought you would have liked wedding planning with your mother more than this." I snapped my head to look at him surprised he even knew of my previous plans. I didn't have time to ask him how he knew though as the smirk on his face ignited the anger from yesterday all over again.

"Do you find my circumstance amusing Mr Taylor?" I challenged him creasing my brow and frowning.

His infuriating smirk stayed put. "I am teasing you Natalie."

"Well forgive me if one of us doesn't find my arranged marriage funny." I paused momentarily. "And you should call me Miss Penhall."

All teasing had gone from his face, now he looked pissed off. "Well Miss Penhall, for the record, I don't find the notion of you marrying *him* funny at all." He spoke the words as if the mere thought of Peter disgusted him. His demeanour had changed from laid back to cold and closed off in seconds, a frosty expression in his eyes. So why was it so damn attractive? Why did I want to wind him up more? The thought of him kissing me like the other night and more ran through my head, I looked at his lips remembering how they felt. Running my tongue lightly over my own and trying to control the intrusive fantasy. I could smell his aftershave; I wanted it to surround me. His body heat rolling off of him despite his chilly attitude. "I'm going to need you to stop looking at me like that, Miss Penhall." His breath fanned down warming my cheeks. We were too close. I took a measured step back glancing around to see if anyone was paying us any attention.

"Are we getting any chickens today?" I asked changing the subject. Only briefly looking at him now hopefully dousing the situation in reality.

"Yes." Was all he replied still staring at me. He didn't move and looked to be thinking something over, staying like that for a few more moments. He snapped out of it. "Would you like to choose them?" He asked me plainly, turning away from me.

"You trust me to?" I raised an eyebrow.

"Of course, unless you make a terrible choice." He teased as we continued down the aisles like our exchange hadn't just happened.

My father caught up to us just as I had picked some hens. He apologised for being held up, I was just glad for a third wheel. Finally relaxing again. "How are we getting on?" He asked looking at us both.

Luke answered on our behalf. "Great, Miss Penhall has just chosen three hens for the flock." He gestured to the cage in front of us.

"Buff Orpington's, eh? You have a good eye Natalie!"

"Hmm, I was steered in the right direction quite a bit." Happy with the compliment even if Luke had to explain every chicken breed to me. Father sorted out the final details with the seller, getting his ticket for collection later on and immediately passing it to Luke.

We spent the next few hours walking around the livestock area. There wasn't a plan to purchase lots of animals today but both men still took the time to go through each section.

Explaining to me the good and bad things to look out for and which type would suit the needs of our farm best. I drank it all in and just when I thought my brain could handle no more information my father stopped our tour. "Right." He clasped his hands together checking his watch. "I think it's time I went and picked the bull for this year."

"Are we not joining you?" I asked.

"No, and I have a confession to make as well. Mr Taylor here was the one who convinced me to let you come along today." I looked between the two men, my heart sinking at the thought that my father hadn't wanted me here at all. I was also questioning why Luke would stick his neck out to convince him otherwise.

"Oh, um." I tried to think of a response, but my tone revealed the disappointment I felt.

"Try not to misunderstand me Natalie, I have enjoyed today and I'm glad he did convince me to let you come along." He paused looking at Luke and then back to me. "Mr Taylor mentioned you learning to ride again but you don't have your own horse. So I, or rather he, thought you might like to go to the horse show and pick one." Another pause. "Only if you would like to though."

Luke interjected. "We can look at the colts and stallions if you want, a male horse might be easier for you." He understood my need to not replace Cinnamon, and I was truly touched by the gesture. I could have hugged him if my father wasn't around. I nodded my head slightly smiling now.

"I would love that, thank you, both of you." We made our way into the tent where they would show the horses, and both took a place standing near the front. Luke leaned forward on the metal barrier whilst I stood awkwardly by his side. Alone again. "So, this was all your idea?" I looked at him nervously waiting for him to reply. He took a moment before responding.

"I've been a prick to you, especially about the learning to ride thing, but also the rest of the time it seems. I guess I was nervous to be alone with you or around you. I don't think I trusted myself to not act on how I felt." He gave me a sly grin. "I didn't want to risk my position at the estate, but that kind of happened anyway."

"We're alone together now."

"Yes, we are." He turned to face me fully not breaking eye contact.

"And do you trust yourself?" I smiled feigning innocence.

"I'm sure I can behave myself with hundreds of people around," He spoke but his eyes finally broke contact to look at my lips before sweeping back up to mine.

"What a shame." I replied coyly just as the first horses were being called out, turning my attention to the ring. I watched as the first few trotted out narrated by a man reading details on each one. I couldn't focus on what he was saying as a warm body pressed against mine pinning me against the railing.

"It is a shame." His voice low, his breath hot on my neck. "If I hadn't promised your dad I would find you a horse." He ran a hand lightly down my arm that was gripping the railing. "I could have shown you how to misbehave. Good job I'm a man of my word, and you're such a good girl you'd never disobey Daddy, would you?" I closed my eyes trying not to get swept away in my fantasy, any moment I felt I could turn and jump him. Hundreds of people watching or not. Then his body was gone, the cold air felt arctic and lonely. I opened my eyes, but he was already back at the railing leaning as if he'd been there the whole time. There was now a cheeky smile on his face, I scowled at him in response.

"Tease." I muttered though I know he heard me. His smile widened and he jerked his head to the ring. I followed his notion and looked at the horses currently out in the ring. "What if I pick a bad one?"

"You just focus on finding one you like, I'll let you know if it's a no-go." He pulled a wad of paper from his back pocket and opened them up. Seeing me looking he spoke. "Details on the horses today, most sellers post about them online prior to the show so I printed them off." He flicked his eyes from the paper to the ring matching up horses as he went. I stared at him in complete wonder. The lengths he had gone to, to make me happy, I could've cried. "Miss Penhall, you should be picking a horse." He scolded not bothering to lift his eyes from his task.

We watched as group after group of horses trotted out and around the paddock. Although Luke mentioned more than a few that were suitable I had yet to see any that I wanted immediately. I was beginning to doubt whether I would find one when the next group was led out. He was third out, a beautiful dark grey covering his head and following down his neck. Midway down his back, the grey stopped exploding into near-white with dark spots. Luke must have seen me craning my neck to get a better look because he began to shuffle his papers finding what he was looking for.

"Dark grey, Appaloosa gelding," He spoke, and I continued to stare at the horse waiting for him to say he wasn't suitable. Gnawing on my lip I sneaked a look at Luke. He looked slightly doubtful, and my heart sank. "He will need some training, and it might be a little while before you can ride him, but I think we can make him work for you." I squealed clasping my hands together.

"What now?" I looked back to the ring where the horses were leaving. Luke nodded in the general direction.

"We go and find the seller."

"OK." I grabbed his arm and started pulling him through the crowd. I lost grip in the throng of people but managed to snag his hand and drag him along. Outside of the tent, we spotted the seller putting the horse back in his mini-paddock. I made our way to him and only when Luke was introducing us did I notice I still had hold of his hand. I released it sheepishly a blush growing on my cheeks. Settling with the owner we then made our way to the loading field. My father seeing us approach came over to greet us.

"Did you pick a bull?"

He waved my question off "Yes, a very nice one. More importantly, did you pick a horse?"

"I did indeed, and he's perfect, isn't he?" I beamed looking at Luke to confirm this. He didn't spare me a glance though and spoke straight to my father.

"He's of good stock, in need of some training. A good fit for Miss Penhall though." He excused himself and went to help load the boxes with the others. My father following to continue his conversation with one of the sellers. I stared at Luke's retreating frame. Frowning slightly at his sudden change, I know he had to be proper in front of my father, but he did that earlier without completely blanking me. Now it was like being anywhere near me was a sin. I huffed and made my way to the car; my emotions couldn't take any more today.

13
Natalie

I tossed and turned in my bed unable to sleep. Throwing the covers off with a dissatisfied huff I got up and put on a pair of slippers. I grabbed a cardigan from the back of a chair and made my way to the kitchen. Flicking on the light I looked at the clock, 1 am. Getting a glass of water I stood at the sink sipping it and looking through the dark window, the path down the garden illuminated by mini solar lights. I hope my horse is doing OK. He needed a name, but I hadn't thought of one that suited him yet, maybe that's what I'll do. If I can't sleep, I might as well go and see if he's OK maybe even come up with a name for him while I'm at it. And to be honest I needed something else to think about other than Luke and how I felt after our encounters yesterday. Grabbing an apple from the fruit bowl I stepped out into the dark.

Wandering down the path I pulled the cardigan tighter around myself. Despite it being July, a cold breeze wrapped around my legs chilling them through the satin fabric of my pyjamas. The inside of the stable was dimly lit and considerably warmer than outside. A few lights were on and the sounds of the horses in their stalls was comforting. I padded along the row of stalls until I reached his. He raised his head as I approached but made no move towards me.

Resting my arms on the door I watched him for a few moments, he didn't seem too bothered by my presence.

"What do you want your name to be? I mean it has to be something strong and proud. How could someone not have named you already?" I half spoke to the statuesque horse and half to myself. Holding out the apple I lightly called for him to come over, but he didn't move. I resigned to tossing it into the stall hoping my peace offering would warm him towards me.

"He's settling in OK." The voice behind me made me jump and I let out a small, startled squeak. Turning to my right I looked at the owner of the voice. Luke was standing a few feet away. "Sorry." He apologised holding up his hands though the corner of his mouth twitched with a smile. I glanced back into the stall.

"I think he's scared of me."

"Nah, he will just take some settling in, has he got a name yet?"

I sighed shaking my head. "I can't seem to think of one, and he's so beautiful it needs to be perfect."

Luke smiled at me. "You'll think of something, try not to stress about it and I'm sure it'll come." He looked down the barn. "It's uh warmer in the office I was just going to make a drink if you want one?"

I nodded at him "Sure." Following him towards the little room at the rear of the barn, when something occurred to

118

me. "Wait, why are you here so late?" He didn't stop walking as he replied to me.

"I wanted to make sure he would be OK, and I wasn't feeling like I could sleep so I figured I might as well stay here."

"That makes sense," as I spoke, he turned his head to look at me, "I couldn't sleep either, so had the same idea."

Luke was right the office was much warmer, the large brown sofa that usually had a farmhand drinking tea on was now occupied by some blankets and piled-up pillows. I went over to an old armchair and sat down, enjoying the smell of leather that came with the comfy perch. Luke was over at the desk, he pulled open a drawer revealing a bottle of whisky. Grabbing some glasses from the small sideboard he poured us both a reasonable measure. He placed mine in my hands before sitting on the corner of the wooden desk and sipping his own. A tense silence settled between us, and I cradled my drink not entirely sure how to break it.

"So, did your mum forgive you?" I looked at Luke who had beaten me to a conversation starter. I frowned slightly.

"No, I don't think so. She's communicating to me solely through Maria." A wry smile crept onto my lips, taking a sip of the amber liquid I continued. "Though I shouldn't complain, at least she isn't going on about..." I let the words fade suddenly sure I didn't want to finish that sentence.

"Your wedding." He finished it for me coldly addressing the elephant in the room. I looked at him finding that I couldn't break his stare but desperately wanting to be free of the scrutiny I saw harboured there.

"Luke, I…"

"What? Forgot you were engaged?" The weather in his tone remained frosty. The echo of the Luke I met when I got home flashed in his face.

"I'm not engaged."

"Pretty sure it doesn't count for much when you're the only one that thinks that. I mean is that what you're going to say when you get in your dress? When you walk down the aisle. Will you tell yourself 'It's not real' on your wedding night?" I knew he was lashing out his voice remained quiet, but the argument was still brewing at the edges. All my frustrations I had bubbling inside me, the pity, the anger and the embarrassment of my situation now threatening to break through my carefully constructed facade. So, I let it.

"I am trying, OK? I don't *want* to be tied to that man. I don't *want* to get married! I don't *want* to live someone else's idea of my life!" My voice had risen, and I stood from my chair placing my glass down as I did so. "Believe it or not I am allowed to want things for myself that differ from my parents. And you! You can think whatever you want! You might think you are the only one hurting, or the only one annoyed at this absolute shit pile of a situation but you are not. I promise you that whatever you are feeling isn't a patch on how I feel! It's my life being dictated. It's my body that is being bargained away. It's me that will have to survive the decisions made by others. At the end of all this, I will be the one losing the most!"

I barely noticed that tears had spilt in betraying streaks down my face. I expected him to berate me, yell back, maybe even laugh, but he did none of those. Instead, he, without commentary, placed his drink down walked across the room to me and wiped a tear from my cheek. I averted my gaze not wanting him to witness the aftermath of my episode or how much it was truly affecting me.

"I'm sorry," He spoke lowly. I raised my eyes shocked to have heard him apologise. His hand still on my cheek it rubbed a light circle there.

"Why?" I sounded quiet as a mouse now. If I wasn't emotionally reeling from my rant, I might have found the will to be ashamed.

"I can't seem to stop being a dick to you."

"I've not exactly been the easiest person to get along with." I tried a smile, but it didn't quite reach.

"Maybe not, but I've definitely made a bad situation worse."

"I don't want to fight with you," I muttered enjoying the comfort I got from having him so close. His hand still on my cheek, he bought his forehead to mine closing his eyes.

"Me neither," He spoke lowly his breath fanning my face.

"We do seem to be pretty good at it though." I sighed wishing with everything that I could have him and the life I wanted to live. The tears threatened my eyes again, but I pushed them back. This man made me want to scream at him, but I would break every rule to stay in this office with his head against mine. So, I made the easiest decision I had in weeks. I leaned up and kissed him, light and unsure. He could push me away; I was after all doing the exact thing I told him not to. But I hoped he wouldn't. His eyes opened in surprise, but it disappeared into lust. Pulling me closer to him he deepened the kiss, I let my eyes flutter closed and put a hand through his hair.

Luke lifted me gently but swiftly and sat me on the edge of the desk. He slightly moved the hem of my silk camisole, his finger brushing my still-raw hip. I hid the sting I felt, futile really as he would see it soon enough if we carried on down this road. Shedding my cardigan, he kissed along my collarbone raising the material ever higher pulling away only to fully remove the article. His lips were on me in an instant. He placed a soft kiss across each breast, my nipples pebbled from the cold and my arousal. There was nothing rushed or desperate in his actions, he was taking his time enjoying me. Luke pulled away from me and I opened my eyes to look at him. His didn't meet mine. Instead, he stared at the bruise sitting in shame on my side. The welts from Peter's fingernails had gone down but not disappeared. A rainbow of bruising was left, ugly and yellowed. My discarded top below me on the floor was of little use, I instead covered the mark with my hands. Luke reached out moving them gently despite his sudden cold demeanour.

"What the fuck is that?" His voice was low almost whispering but the anger and accusation was still audible.

"Um..." My mind fumbled over what to say and my body wanted to hide. Perched topless I couldn't care less about my breasts being on display I just wanted to hide that damn bruise. I didn't know what to say to make Luke understand, to not see me as weak. He looked at me expectantly his expression serious and questioning. "Peter..." It was the only word I could croak out. He exhaled stepping back from me. Anger twisting his gorgeous features until he looked outright scary.

"Stay here." he turned and started for the door. My mind snapping free with his action. I got down from the desk and grabbed his arm before he could reach it.

"Don't." I pleaded with him.

"Don't defend him Natalie." He was furious pain swilling through the anger in his eyes.

"I'm not. I just don't want to ruin this." I was nearly begging him now.

"Did he? I mean what he said the other day… did he?" Luke was studying my expression trying to find his answers before I gave them. My mind stuttered briefly trying to understand what he meant, when it dawned on me. What Peter had said he would do to me given the chance.

"No! God no! Luke, he didn't he…" I tried to get all the reassurance out at once, my words clashing but needing

Luke to know he hadn't forced me or fulfilled any of his vile threats. "He just hurt me, it doesn't hurt too much anymore." He looked both relieved and still angry.

"He shouldn't…"

"Shhh, I know, but he's not here now. This is me and you. I don't want to think about him, at all" I pulled him close to me again trying to comfort his anger. Moving my hand from his cheek down to his arm. I place light kisses along his neck. He sighed moving to give me better access. Running my finger along his waist until I found his belt buckle. My hands worked on the fastening undoing it then his jeans, pulling them down until he sprung free of the fabric. I kept my eyes on his watching as the last threads of rage warred with the desire creeping in. As my fingers found his length his eyes closed, and I felt him grow harder in my palm. I worked him slowly savouring the moment, teasing him like he had with me. Softly brushing my thumb over the head letting his pre-cum slick the digit. I stopped my torture to work on removing his shirt, mesmerised by the sight of his chest being slowly revealed to me. Carved, rough and tanned from working hard in the sun. I ran my tongue over my lip, wanting to run it down his muscles, but chose to follow the pace he had set and make him wait.

He was patient with me, watching my every movement intently, letting me explore and enjoy myself but I wanted him to take control. I needed him to chase his desire. I leaned up so my lips brushed his neck just under his ear, I whispered. "So are you going to help me forget all about him?" It was all I needed to provoke him. Grabbing the back of my neck he kissed me like he was dying of thirst, and I was his oasis. I felt the hot heavy desperation roll off of him, like if he just kissed me hard enough Peter would disappear. I put my hands on his sides to steady myself. He backed us up to the desk and with a broad motion swept the contents onto the floor, pushing me back until I was sprawled on the now bare wood. His eyes roamed down my body before flicking to mine.

"Do you want me to continue where I left off?" I nodded at him trying my best not to blush. "Use your words Natalie."

"Yes...please" I breathed out, shocked that I still had the use of my voice while my brain had vacated.

"Good girl." He placed one softer kiss on my lips before moving south. He sucked a nipple into his mouth swirling his tongue over the bud before pulling on it with his teeth. I gasped at the painful pleasure and grabbed a fistful of his hair. His tongue danced and played over one nipple while his fingers pinched and teased the other. I moaned greedily pushing my chest into him. His mouth swapped to my other side leaving his hands free to remove my trousers. He trailed a finger along my bikini line sending an involuntary shiver up my body. His finger moving slowly between my folds soaking it immediately with how wet I was. He groaned against me the vibrations caressing my nipple. He released the mound with a pop before getting on his knees at the end of the desk. He grabbed my legs pulling me closer to the edge before burying his face between them. It took all my strength not to explode immediately. He sucked and lapped at me drawing me closer and closer to the precipice. "Let go baby." He all but ordered and I did. Crashing over the edge my body trembling. He held onto my thighs consuming me as I came. He moved back to my lips letting me taste myself on his tongue, and damn if I didn't taste good.

"I need you Luke," I whispered against his lips. Grasping his cock between us letting him know exactly what I wanted. I didn't need to ask twice. He moved the head to my entrance pausing to look at me.

"Are you on anything? I don't have a…" He looked unsure.

"Yes, I am." never more thankful for that than right now. He smiled and finally eased into me. I felt instantly full, I wasn't sure I would last long like this either.

"Fuck." He sighed out. He started slow letting me adjust. It was torture.

"Faster Luke…. Please." I didn't care that I was begging, I didn't want him to hold back.

"So impatient." he smiled at me but sped up. Finding his rhythm, he grabbed my legs up to his shoulder slamming into me. The new angle had me building again, my nails digging into the wood of the desk. I bit my lip muffling my voice to a hot whimper, not convinced on the barn being very soundproof. "I can't hold on much longer Natalie." His words had me tumbling constricting his length inside me as I came around him. He thrust a few more times before finding his release burying himself even deeper in me.

He removed himself before gently placing my legs down. "Wait there." He quickly strode to the other side of the

126

room grabbing a cloth and wetting it from the tap before returning. He rubbed the cool material over me cleaning up the mess we made. My overly sensitive area making me shudder. Once he was done, he placed a soft kiss to my head before grabbing my pyjamas for me and redressing himself.

I stood looking at the mess we had made. Scattered paper and stationery littered the floor. I giggled behind my hand, before bending down to scoop up a few items. Before I could grab a second lot, Luke grasped my hands.

"I'll clean that up." his voice was gentle and calm. He looked more relaxed than I had seen him. I wanted to giggle again or swell with pride, knowing I had helped him relax filled me with happiness.

"Are you sure?" I stared at the piles of stuff.

"Absolutely, it's late you should get some rest."

I glanced at the clock on the wall it was gone three. "Yes probably." I sighed not wanting this night to end, not knowing when and if we would get to be together again.

"I'll walk you back." He moved to the door.

I stopped him as I spoke. "Probably not a good idea." he looked at me offended for a moment. "I meant it Luke I'm not jeopardising your position here."

He sighed knowing I was right. He looked at the floor before scooping up a piece of paper and a pen. He scribbled on it before handing it to me. "My number. Text me when you're back in the house." I didn't know my heart could grow any fonder of this man, but I beamed at him when he handed me the note.

"I will." I gave him one last brief kiss before leaving.

Back in my bed I quickly added Luke's number into my phone and dropped him a text.

In bed safe. x

He replied almost instantly.

Good. Sweet dreams Natalie xx

I didn't think I would sleep, I still felt high on Luke and the night we had had. But I succumbed quickly, my mind finally resting.

14
Luke

The sun rising slowly painted the office in a golden glow. I hadn't slept after Natalie had returned to the house, choosing instead to finish some paperwork. It had been slow going though. I couldn't stop thinking about last night, how amazing it had felt to just be with her. There was also the not-so-small matter of what Peter had done. I had tried not to think about it too much, every time I did my fingers twitched for a fight. Plagued by the anger coupled with the fact I couldn't even walk her to her door. When that pathetic excuse could do as he pleased. I knew Lord Penhall would be furious to know what he had done but Natalie wasn't going to tell him anytime soon. And there was no way for me to explain how I had seen it. Looking at the time and seeing it was already 5.30 I decided to pay a last visit to our new resident before heading home.

The horse with no name was calm in his stall, he had settled in pretty well. The trust would come later. For now, he kept to himself unsure of all of us out here. I was just leaving the stables when I bumped into Mike. "You're here early," I remarked to him.

"So are you." He laughed.

"Actually, I'm here late and I'm heading home now." I explained, he gave me a quizzical look. "I stayed with the new intake, wanted to make sure he was OK." I added more information. Running a hand through my hair the tiredness catching up with me as the morning breeze hit my face.

"I see. Well go get some rest lad, I'll keep an eye on him today."

Thanking him I started for home. I usually loved my morning walk to work but the return journey after a sleepless and active night left me wiped out and definitely ready to surrender to my bed.

Knocking had me prying my eyes open. I look at my bedside, 10 am, this better be important. I grabbed some shorts tugging them roughly on and stomping downstairs. I had only been asleep for a few hours, if this was one of the guys, I hope they had their affairs in order. I unlatched the door swinging it open with aggravated force that it didn't need. I glared at the disturber for only a second before realising who it was. Natalie. "What are you doing here?" My voice must have sounded gruff because she stopped smiling and looked very unsure. "Sorry." I apologised quickly. "I was asleep." Her eyes widened.

"Oh my gosh, I'm sorry Luke, I didn't even think of the time. I just. Well, I was busy today, but I pulled a sickie on my parents. I wanted to talk to you. To tell you. Or to ask you." She was babbling and looking very flustered. Cute. Suddenly I didn't care that she had woken me up. I looked around my small front yard, this was bold of her, anyone might have seen. She was still babbling when I grabbed her arm, effectively pulling her into my house. "Oof." She let out a small release of air as she fell into my chest. She looked up at me through her lashes having finally shut up.

"Coffee?" I released her and made my way into the kitchen. I figured it best not to wait for an answer, she, and I, clearly needed one.

"Y-yes?" I shook my head at her answer, that sounded more like a question. Smiling to myself wondering how she went from the quick-tongued minx ready to chew me out to a nervous wreck.

"What did you want to talk about?" I asked turning from the coffee pot.

"Huh?" She scraped her eyes up my naked top half before answering. Oh, so you like what you see? I crossed my arms over my chest flexing my biceps slightly, I know cheap move. But very worth it to see the blush and shy smile form on her face. "About last night." She began, and I didn't like the tone.

I braced myself for the guilty excuse, waiting for her to say we made a mistake. I didn't want it to be a one-off, Christ I don't think I could handle it if it was a one-off. I turned back to our mugs I didn't want her to read the worry in my face. "What about it?" I tried to sound nonchalant, I wasn't sure if I failed.

"Well, I know we can't be together, my parents would never allow it. Not to mention what they would do to you. I can't give you what you want or deserve. I can't go out to dinners with you. I can't meet you for lunch or take trips to the cinema. We probably couldn't grab a coffee in public without arousing suspicion." I was stone as she spoke. Staring at the coffee trying not to let my heart break. "I can't give you all those things and I see no way of this working. But I want to try anyway." She stopped, clearly waiting for my response.

Turning to face her I could see she was serious. "You want to try?" My brain wouldn't comprehend what she was saying. I wanted to act like a giddy schoolboy, pick her up and spin her around but the surprise kept me rooted in place. I was in shock.

She nodded lightly, closing the gap between us. "Maybe, until I figure my mess of a life out, we can try and find a normal that works for us. Luke, I want to be with you and I'm willing to try anything to make it happen." YES, YES YES! I clasped her face in my hands and kissed her, placing endless kisses on her lips. She giggled against them, her infectious smile spreading to my own face. "I take it that means you want to as well?" She spoke in-between pecks.

"Seriously? You need to ask?" I pulled back giving her a lopsided grin and raising my eyebrows at her. Were my kisses not answer enough?

"Well, I don't know you might have not wanted to after…"

"After what?" I frowned.

132

"Last night." She twiddled her fingers. "You might not have wanted me anymore."

"Do you think I would only want you for sex?"

She blushed deeply. "Well, I don't know. Maybe. I didn't want you to feel obligated for more if that's all you wanted from me."

"For a smart girl, you're being kind of dumb." She looked taken aback. "I told you how I feel, and it wasn't just a line to get you naked." I paused showing her I was sincere. "OK?"

She nodded "OK." Stepping back and looking me over she added. "You should probably go back to bed though; I still woke you up."

I shrugged. "Nah, not tired anymore." It was true I was too hyped up to sleep now. "Bed does sound good though." I winked at her.

Tutting she slapped my arm; I caught her wrist before it retracted pulling her into me again. The kiss I gave her this time was softer, slower and promising. I felt her melt into me, relaxing finally and just existing with me in this moment. I never wanted to let her go. I did, however. Handing her the coffee which she took with thanks and leading her into the living room. I sat on the large sofa, and she positioned herself right next to me. Perfect.

"How was my boy this morning?" She asked taking a sip of the hot liquid.

133

"He was OK, I think it will take him a while to settle in fully. But if you visit him regularly and start building that bond, I'm sure it will come quickly." She nodded at what I was saying.

"I'll go down every day if I can." It was great how excited she was and the added bonus of her being at the stables every day was not lost on me.

"That would be good. He can get to know you better if you do that." I agreed with her plan.

"You'll be around too?" She glanced at me over her mug.

"I guess." I looked at her lips as they caught a lingering taste of coffee. "Is that OK?"

Wrinkling her nose, she shrugged a shoulder. "I suppose."

"Oh, you suppose, well then I shall make myself scarce when you visit."

"No don't." She didn't sound convincingly worried but serious all the same.

"If you want me there, I'll be there."

"I want you there." She almost whispered back. I took the mug out of her hands placing it on the table next to mine. Scooping her up I put her in my lap, and she straddled my waist. The thin fabric of my shorts not much of a barrier between me and her. I didn't want her to think I was only interested in the physical, sitting down with her to purposefully have a conversation. But right now, I just wanted to feel her again. She dipped her head down to kiss me, her hair creating a curtain between us and the rest of the world. She ground her hips down, eliciting a tortured moan from me. She tried to hide her proud smirk.

"If you don't stop that, I'm going to fuck you right here." I warned her, though I was hoping she would let me see good on it. Still smirking she stood from my lap. I was fixated on her as she moved, her eyes never leaving mine.

"Maybe I'll fuck you right here." She didn't wait for me to respond before removing her t-shirt. Slower with her jeans she popped the button open and began sliding them down her hips, inch by inch. They fell to the floor leaving her in a lacy red underwear set. If I wasn't hard before then I was like steel now.

Falling to her knees between my legs she gently parted them wider. Running her hands up my calves, her nails lightly scratching the skin. I sucked in a breath as her fingers found my waistband. Lifting my hips slightly as she pulled, letting her tug the clothing fully off. She grasped my cock in her hands, gently stroking it. Her hands moving to the tip which she ran a finger over. I swallowed some of my lust, watching her work our eyes never breaking.

With a final small smile at me, she moved and ran her lips up the path her hand was taking. Heading back down she flicked out her tongue licking the full length, her eyes closed like it was her favourite ice cream on a hot summer day. I let my head fall back on the sofa as she repeated the torture. Tasting every inch of me. I snapped my eyes back to her when she took me into her mouth, taking almost all of me before pulling back up. Letting me escape with a satisfying pop. I watched her as she took me again and again. One hand working my base while the other moved between her legs to please herself. Fuck. I was ready to bust but I wanted her pussy. I needed to feel how wet she was for me. Just when I thought I couldn't hold any longer she stopped. Picking herself up she moved back to my lap, hovering over my more than ready cock.

"Do you want me to fuck you?" She asked in a voice that was all false innocence.

"Stop teasing and sit your pretty ass down." I commanded her. She let out a small giggle but did as she was told, sliding down me with ease. She paused when she reached the hilt, taking a deep breath and letting herself get comfortable. Not lingering she slid her body back up before moving down with more force this time. Crying out slightly. She picked up the pace drawing every moan she could, taking what she needed from me. I placed a finger over her swollen clit, strumming it in time with her bouncing.

"Luke, I'm gonna, I'm…"

"That's it baby, cum for me." I goaded her release helping her chase the euphoria. She came around me, her thighs squeezing my hips. I grasped her pounding into her, not lasting much longer before I joined her high. Collapsing onto me I held her as she shook slightly. Her head in the crook of my neck as I stroked her back, bringing her down.

136

I felt her breath on my neck as she spoke. "Shall we shower?"

I didn't need asking twice. I scooped her up placing a kiss on her nose. "You soaking wet and covered in soap, I'm there!" I took us upstairs as she laughed.

15
Natalie

"We're having dinner tonight."

I had just arrived home after spending a wonderful morning with Luke. I insisted he went back to bed and despite him trying to persuade me to join him I had stayed firm. I did ask if I could come back this evening, he happily agreed to the compromise.

Having stepped into the foyer to find Peter there, my happiness balloon had deflated a little. His statement then puncturing whatever remained.

"I have plans tonight," I replied removing my shoes.

"Cancel them." He ordered, his mouth a thin line.

I was about to retort when my mother entered from the sitting room. "Oh good Natalie you're home, Peter, have you told her?"

"I have my Lady." His tone was charming with a matching set smile now on his face.

"Wonderful!" My mother looked too excited; it unsettled me. Just like when she had first introduced me to Peter, I could tell she knew something I did not.

"I was just explaining to Mr Layton that regrettably I already have plans this evening." I explained again to my mother keeping my face friendly.

She huffed back at me, pursing her lips. "Don't be rude Natalie, your plans can wait." I went to protest but closed my mouth again when she shot me a glare. Sighing in defeat I made my way to the stairs.

"I must change, call me when dinner is ready."

Peter spun on his heel following the direction of my movements. "Actually, we are going out to dinner, just us."

I flicked my eyes between my mother and Peter. This felt like a trap. "When?"

"We leave at seven." Checking his watch.

"Fine." I retreated to my room. Opening my phone I text Luke, apologising that I wouldn't be able to make it back tonight. I suspected he was asleep as he didn't reply.

We arrived at the restaurant; 'Tallulah' written above the door in gold lettering. The driver opened my door and Peter was already waiting to take my arm. I felt extremely uncomfortable but at least we were in public. Other people equalled safety. Leading us inside it was all gold and black décor. Much darker than I was expecting, given the light summer evening we had entered from. We were promptly seated by the maître d', Peter ordering wine for us both. Ignoring the fact I didn't drink red, and then we were alone. I toyed with my napkin on my lap, trying not to meet Peter's eye. He sipped his wine before addressing me.

"You look, nice tonight." There was a pause in his compliment and I smiled knowing he hated what I was wearing. I had chosen the most modest dress in my wardrobe, it had a high neckline and full-length sleeves, the hem sitting at my knee. I hadn't missed his disappointment when I made my entrance earlier. He looked me over finding not an inch of skin over my calves to leer at. It wasn't even a bad dress, nice enough for my mother to compliment me on it with some sincerity but certainly not what Mr Layton would have me wearing. It was slightly plain, and Peter did not like plain, ironically.

"Thank you, as do you." I complimented him back though I couldn't say with confidence if he had even changed his suit since this afternoon. A young server approached our table to take our first-course order. Peter again ordered for both of us, I tried not to let my irritation show.

"Excuse me," I spoke to the waiter just as he turned to go.

"Yes, Miss." He smiled at me; I didn't miss the scowl on Peter's face.

"Could I get a sparkling water, please? With ice. Thank you."

140

Nodding at my request. "Of course." he left us.

Clearing his throat Peter spoke. "So, Natalie how has your weekend been?" the pleasant air to his voice catching me a little off guard.

"It's been quite good thank you, and your own?" I asked being polite but wondering what he was up to. He was too smart to know his faux charms didn't work on me.

"Yes, it's been good." He paused sipping his wine. "What did you get up to? Your mother mentioned on Friday that the two of you would be conducting some wedding planning."

"We didn't get round to it in the end. I accompanied my father to the show on Saturday instead."

"Oh, that's a shame." I couldn't help but think how it wasn't a shame at all. "But I'm sure attending the show was also quite pleasant."

"It was, I had a wonderful time." Choosing not to tell him of Luke's involvement I omitted some details as I continued. "I purchased a new horse, with my lessons going well it was about time I had one of my own."

He nodded. "Perhaps we could go out for a ride sometime?" I couldn't work out why he was being so agreeable all of a sudden.

I smiled. *Perhaps not.*

141

We had finished two courses when the server approached us asking if we would like any dessert. My sweet tooth wasn't going to resist.

"It all sounds good, what would you recommend?" I asked our server.

"The crème Brulé is delicious as is the parfait but personally I adore the chocolate brownie. Triple chocolate and very decadent."

"Well, I absolutely love chocolate." I laughed a little. Peter's face was infuriated. His foot under the table finding my own, my toes bare in the heeled sandals. He pressed his shoe into them, I tried to move my foot back without making a noise, but he just pressed harder making it impossible. "I'll have the brownie please," I spoke to the server not meeting his eye again.

Once he had taken our menus and left Peter finally released my foot. Putting a charmed smile back on he tried to continue conversation. When I didn't respond in the way he wanted he huffed giving up. Standing up abruptly I thought he might be leaving but he instead came round to my side of the table. I did my best not to recall at his proximity. Reminding myself there wasn't much he could do in a busy restaurant.

"Might as well get this over with," He muttered and I'm not sure whether I was supposed to hear him. All my curiosity stopped when he got down on one knee. Every eye in the room was now on us a few excited gasps falling from our audience's lips. I could cry, everyone would assume they were tears of happiness, but they wouldn't come. The shock taking over everything else. He pulled a small blue box from his jacket pocket, opening it to reveal a huge, gaudy, diamond ring. "Natalie Elizabeth Penhall, will you marry me?" He looked at me expectantly. *No no no no.* I was frozen unable to reject or accept. He took the ring from the box, tossing the latter onto the table he grabbed my left hand. Roughly he pushed the jewellery down my finger scraping the skin off of it for good measure. I winced but didn't have time to protest before he kissed me. The prick actually kissed me, on the lips, in front of the entire restaurant. He didn't release my hand as he sat back down forcing me to reach across the table. I must have been white as a sheet, I certainly felt sick. "Smile" He hissed though he barely opened his mouth.

I forced a smile onto my face, even though I knew it wouldn't look sincere. The server arrived back with our desserts a beaming smile on his face. "On the house for the happy couple." He chirped placing them and taking his leave.

We finished them in silence Peter having given me back my left hand. I maintained my composure despite the fact I was seething. He wore a smug smile on his face, he thinks this means he has won. We continued our quiet game all the way home. He accompanied me into the house; I couldn't be bothered to stop him. I doubt he would have listened anyway.

143

As soon as the door was closed my mother appeared making me jump as she clapped her hand squealing with happiness. She should have gotten engaged; her reactions were much better than my own. Pulling my hand to her she looked at the ring beaming me a smile that screamed '*you lucky girl*'. I stared at her blankly. "It's official! We should celebrate, I'll get the drinks and your father. Where is he?" She started looking around, I took the opportunity to release myself from her grasp.

"I'm going to retire for the night."

"Nonsense Natalie you must join the toast you're the bride-to-be!" I wanted to laugh and cry at her words.

"Mother, it's been an emotional day and I need to rest. Plan a proper celebration when you find father." I didn't give her time to reply heading for the stairs and straight to my room.

Closing and locking the door I slid to the floor pulling off my shoes, evaluating the damage done to my toes. They were still hurting, and the top of my foot was a flared red. I don't think he managed to break them thankfully. Finishing with my foot I went to my hand next. Pulling the ring off I thought of tossing it in the bin, that would probably lead to more problems later. I placed it back in its box, putting it on my bathroom vanity. I would just put it on in front of my mother. The abrasion on my ring finger wasn't as bad as my toes, I soaked it in the sink effectively cooling it off.

Grabbing my phone, I sent a quick message to Luke.

Are you awake? x

144

Hey, yes. x

His reply was almost instant. I smiled instantly feeling better than I had all night.

Want some company? x

My phone rang not a moment later, I answered it Luke's husky voice coming down the line.

"I always want your company."

I tried not to blush, but he had me heating up with that one line. "OK, I shall sneak out in a bit."

"I'll come get you," He spoke, and I could hear him moving.

"You don't have to do that." I began to protest.

"Yes I do, it's pitch black out. Don't worry I won't be seen. Meet me by the hedge maze in 15?"

"OK."

I hung up, quickly changing out of my dress into much more comfortable clothes and trainers. I knew that no one would hear or see me if I took the back stairwell. So that's what I did, poking my head out of my room to check first, I could hear conversation far within the house. I locked my bedroom door behind me in case my mother decided to come up and cajole me for not joining in any celebrations.

I made it to the back door unseen, stepping out into the warm night I walked straight to the maze. Trying to steady my beating heart against the excitement it felt. I didn't wait long before footsteps on the gravel alerted me to someone coming. For a moment I considered it might be someone from the house, I looked for a hiding spot in case it was. Putting myself behind a large urn.

"Natalie?" I heard Luke whisper call. Stepping out from behind the pot seeing him now only a few metres away. "What are you doing behind there?" He laughed at me.

"Hiding, I wasn't sure it was you." I felt a little embarrassed. He closed the distance grabbing my arms and kissing my cheek.

"Did you have a good evening?"

"Not really." I shrugged trying not to get upset over the day's events.

"What did you get up to?" He continued taking my hand in his and walking us back the way he had come.

"Dinner...with Satan." I muttered the last part.

"He made the trip especially from hell?" He laughed a little, though I could tell it was only for my benefit. "Did you want to talk about it?"

I shook my head no. "I'd rather forget about it."

"I think I can help with that." He pulled me to him, kissing me deeply. I pulled him closer helping him to help me. He grabbed my thighs lifting me and I wrapped them around his waist. We were out of sight of the manor now, the tall trees and hedges guarding us from any prying eyes. He pulled away from my lips placing kisses along my collarbone.

"Are you planning to have sex with me everywhere except your bed?" I teased him.

He stopped looking me in the eyes his expression serious. "No…I'm planning to have sex with you everywhere, including my bed." He smirked before kissing me again. I giggled against his lips. I pouted when he put me down. Letting him instead lead me back to his house.

16
Natalie

I ran through the manor, grasping Luke's hand and pulling him with me. There was no one but us home. My parents had gone to London for a few days and Maria had the day off. Any other members of staff will have finished their work by now and not be back until tomorrow. Luke had been against this idea when I suggested it this morning, stating that it was asking to get caught. One semi-naked picture of me later and he changed his tune. I had laid on my bed giggling with excitement, now he was here I wasn't going to waste any time.

"So, this is your room?" He looked around when I finally halted inside the suite. "Can I get a tour?"

"Wardrobe, bathroom, bedroom." I gestured around the room before placing my hands on his shirt pulling him into me. I kissed him lightly.

He laughed pulling back from me. "You're so impatient."

"Would you rather keep a lady waiting?" I batted my eyelashes, popping the button on my jeans. His eyes wandered down my body following my movements.

148

"No ma'am." He stepped forward picking me up, my legs wrapping around him he walked us to the bed. He threw me backwards, and I hit the soft mattress. Standing at the end of the bed he pulled off each of my shoes and socks not breaking eye contact. I perched on my elbows watching him watch me. "Take off your top Natalie." I didn't need to be told twice. I pulled it up over my head, probably looking ridiculous as I desperately scrabbled to remove the fabric. I didn't care. His hands, circling my ankles, grabbed the cuffs of my jeans. I leaned my hips up slightly allowing him to tug them off. Still fully dressed he stood back from me. Staring down at my naked form his eyes lit a path of heat as they roamed my body. His tongue flicked across his bottom lip like he was imagining the taste of me. He removed his top, his muscles flexing as the material was lifted from himself. I bit my lip trying to control my desire. Removing his jeans and his boxers he stood proudly naked. He palmed his already hard length, still watching me. I tried to maintain eye contact, my gaze betraying me as it swayed to his pelvis and his hand working on himself.

"Touch yourself." His voice was low and smooth. I flicked my eyes back to him, a little embarrassed at his request. I hesitated unsure of my confidence. The wish to please him won over. My hands, shaking a little moved across my abdomen. I watched his eyes follow the path I was taking, reaching my thigh I teased him for a moment rubbing circles into the skin. Swallowing the very last of my nerves I slipped a finger between myself, instantly wetting it. Letting it glide across my sensitive bud, I found a rhythm. My other hand freely exploring my breasts, I pulled and tweaked at my perked nipples. Drawing small moans from myself.

149

Luke crawled onto the end of the bed, edging further up my body. Rescinding the space between us until his face was hovering over mine, and he was perfectly placed between my legs. I had stopped my own hands to focus on what he was doing. He lifted one hand from the bed snaking it between us, until he found his mark. I waited for him to push into me but he didn't. Instead moving his hand to where mine had just been and teasing the area. He slipped a finger into me, and then another. Curling the long digits, making my breath catch. He worked his fingers in and out at a tortuous pace, his mouth inches from mine whispering words of encouragement.

Slowly drawing me to the edge until I was stumbling ready to fall. "There it is baby. Come on let go for me," he spoke the last few urging words as I came for him. I was still riding the euphoria when he thrust into me. He didn't waste any time, his pace needy and ferocious. His lips finally finding mine. The taste of them splitting through my desire. His hand that had teased my inside now flicked over my clit, pulling me with him until I was ready to fall again.

"I'm close Luke." He moaned at my words. I screamed my release, his lips capturing the sound as he came with me. Caressing my jaw, he placed a last soft kiss on my nose and lips before getting up.

"Which one was the bathroom?" He questioned looking between the doors. I let the sight of his bare behind distract me for a moment before I spoke.

"Left." I also rose from the bed following him in.

150

He flicked on the shower ceremoniously standing aside, sweeping his arm for me to step into the large booth first. I giggled at his exaggerated chivalry. "Aren't you joining me?" I questioned when he closed the glass.

"I will be I'm just going to grab a couple of towels." A pause. "Where do you keep them?"

"In the cupboard to the right of the sink," I replied letting the warm water soak down my muscles. A few moments passed without a response from Luke. "Did you find them?" Nothing. I could see his form through the steamed door but he had his back to me. "Luke?" I called him. Nothing. Furrowing my brow I slid open the door to ask what he was doing. I stepped out the cold air prickling my skin. I placed a hand on his shoulder. He tensed. "Luke, are you OK?" Standing next to him I saw what had caused him to stop. In his hand was my engagement ring. "Oh." The realisation slid from my mouth.

"Yeah, Oh."

"I was going to tell you, but."

"But you didn't." He put the ring back down still looking at it like it was diseased. "Do not lie to me, Natalie."

"I didn't." I stuttered.

"You were never going to tell me," he stated plainly. Having not conjured up the words or conversation I would have had with him, I couldn't deny what he was saying. I wanted to reassure him that I was going to tell him but, in

151

my heart, I didn't know if I was ever going to have been brave enough for that.

"But." I teetered on whether to go down this road but it was the only logic I had. "It doesn't mean anything. I haven't worn it since he put it on. It means nothing to me. It's just him and my mother trying to make this farce of an engagement more real."

"How much more real does it need to be Natalie?" We were back to the same argument, only this time I didn't want to fight. I couldn't even be angry any more. His hurt was justified and his frustrations had more than a solid foundation. But I had nothing to say at least nothing new.

"It isn't real to me. This engagement isn't real. That ring isn't real. The only thing I know is real is you and me. Is this." My eyes were begging but he just looked at me with hurt.
"I can't do this." he walked out of the bathroom. I followed. Picking up clothes and pulling them back on he didn't look at me as I spoke.

"Can't do what?" I grabbed my robe only now noticing my nakedness. I wasn't about to chase him down wearing nothing. "Luke!" I raised my voice a little when he didn't respond.

"I can't wait for the other shoe to drop Nat." He was tugging on his top his face briefly covered by the fabric. When he had it on he looked at me, complete confusion swimming across his face.

"What would you have me do?" A few stray tears fell. "Do you not think I have tried to find a way out of this? Do you not think that getting my parents to see reason doesn't take up half my thoughts?"

"We sneak around because you say you worry for me?!" His voice raised. "You don't care about my job, my life, how it would affect me! You do it for you! You do it because it is your own life you can't bare to lose. You wouldn't dream of throwing all this away!" He swept a hand around the room. Shaking his head he turned from me.

I wouldn't follow him, if that is how he thought of me then I would let him leave. "That's not true." Was all I said before I returned to the bathroom, knowing he would leave, but needing to be away from him. I heard the bedroom door slam a few moments later, the regret was instant.

Luke hadn't replied to a single call or text. It had been four days now. To start with I had tried to get hold of him but after two days of radio silence, I stopped trying. I figured he need space, specifically from me. So, I stopped pushing.

I stood brushing my beautiful boy's mane. 'Argent' had warmed to me now; I was convinced it was because he finally had a name. A soft knock at the stall door had me turning. The small hope I felt squashed when I saw Charlie. I forced a smile going back to grooming.

"Still nothing," He asked. I shook my head not bothering to turn it. "Want to go for a ride?"

"Aren't you working?" I answered his question with one of my own. Looking at him leaning on the frame he gave a half shrug.

"Everyone's preparing for this weekend I doubt they'll even notice."

"This weekend?"

"Ascot?" He spelled out for me looking even more confused.

"Oh shit." I cursed. Knowing I would be going. More to the point knowing I would be going with my parents and Peter.

"Language young lady!" Charlie teased. I feigned throwing my brush at him.

"The ride will have to wait." I brushed my jeans down, breezing past Charlie.

"Good talk!" He shouted after me as I made my way from the barn.

I found Maria quickly, she was busying herself in the laundry room. "Do you know where Mother is?"

"Good morning to you too Natalie."

"Sorry, good morning, Maria." I looked at her expectantly.

She sighed. "In the sunroom, though she has company."

"That's fine," I called as I left. Making my way through the house to the back. The sunroom sitting off of the dining hall. It was a beautiful space full of plants and flowers. "Mother," I announced stepping into the already warming room.

"Oh Natalie, we were just talking about you. Please join us." She motioned to the empty seat. That's when I saw who her company was. Peter.

"Never mind." I curled my lip regarding the man. "I'll speak with you later when you're less occupied."

"Nonsense, sit." She poured me a cup of tea as I shuffled into a seat. "What did you want to discuss?"

"Um Ascot, but it can wait." I waved off the need.

"Oh, that's what we were just discussing." She beamed between the pair of us. "You need to tell Peter what you will be wearing so he can coordinate with you."

"I'm not going." I stated plainly. This was it, my moment to put my foot down.

"Of course you are." My mother rolled her eyes at me searching the ceiling for some unknown willpower she might find there.

"I'd rather not attend this year."

"Well, be that as it may, your presence is required. You are engaged and expecting your fiancé to go alone would be rude."

"I don't have a fiancé." I quipped growing agitated.

"Did he not propose the other night?" She now looked confused.

"I did." It was the first thing Peter had said since my entrance.

"You fail to recall that I did not accept," I replied to him, then to both of them. "A ring roughly shoved on my finger is not an acceptance. I must applaud you for doing it in such a public space, to minimise the chances of me refusing." I paused staring at my mother's shocked face and Peter's angry one. "We aren't in public now though, so I can wholeheartedly say I do not accept."

My mother's laugh was jarring. "That's not up to you dear."

"Yes, it is."

She pursed her lips. "Natalie if that is truly how you feel then I suggest we go to your father right now." She stood addressing Peter. "Mr Layton will you excuse us." He nodded as my mother left. I followed.

"How dare you?" She lectured me once we were out of earshot of the sunroom. "We have done everything for you. You've had everything Natalie. We even sent you to the school of your choice despite my reservations about it being

156

on the other side of the world." She huffed side-eyeing me. "You were happy to take all the privileges, but when it comes to doing your bit. Your duty, you can't be bothered." We had arrived at my father's office; she knocked not waiting before opening the door. "In." She ordered me, following and closing the door.

They were both just staring at me. My mother had told my father and he had listened quietly. Now they both stare mute like a game of chicken, to see who would talk first. I chewed my lip nervously.

"Why?" My father questioned, though when I went to answer he shot me a look, effectively letting me know it was rhetorical. "After everything we have done?" The world fell from beneath me. My mother I could understand she had always been a stickler for image. But him. Lord Penhall. My father. I expected more from him.

"Father, please." He stopped me.

"I can't hear it any more Natalie." He looked at me with disappointment. "Are you not part of this family? Is that not what you want?" I began to doubt whether I did with every word he spoke. "I thought you wanted to be head of this estate, you were born to be the countess and now you are telling me you don't want it."

"I do want it." It was true I did. Luke was right that this is the life I wanted. He was wrong in thinking I wouldn't give it up. "That isn't what I'm arguing, I simply do not wish to marry Mr Layton."

"They are one and the same." He stated. "You will marry him if you wish to continue being a part of this family." His gaze softened slightly. "Arranged marriages are not easy Natalie, but I think you will find they can hold many comforts."

His comfort came too late. I saw the resolution in his eyes. I would play along for now but my days here were numbered. "I am part of this family." In my heart, I knew this wasn't a family I wanted to be a part of anymore. I tried not to let the organ break. A weight settling there that this wasn't where I belonged.

"So, we can expect the rest of this engagement to go smoothly?" He queried, my mother standing by like the cat that got the cream.

Standing I looked between them. "I do not like Mr Layton, nor do I like this arrangement. I will do it with public grace if it's truly what you demand of me?" I let them make their own beds. Solidify what I knew one last time.

"Good." My mother spoke for both of them, my father only nodded. "As I said you need to tell me what you intend to wear this weekend." She ushered me out like the last 20 minutes hadn't happened.

"Of course," I responded dryly. As we walked my mother waffled on about dresses and hats.

My own mind stayed on track, to find a way out.

17
Luke

It had been days since I had seen Natalie last. She had
texted and called a few times, but I had ignored all of the
messages. It was childish I know but I needed head space
and time. I was falling for her more and more every day but
to see that ring. To see that he had proposed, and she had
accepted. It hurt. I know she said she didn't have a choice
and that she hadn't exactly accepted his proposal. But she
had. She had the ring; their wedding was becoming more of
an inevitability.

It was race day today. Ascot. I knew she would be there, but
we wouldn't have to talk to each other. I could do my best
to avoid her. I hadn't figured a way out of this mess yet, and
the next time we spoke I wanted to be able to give her
another option. She wouldn't let me throw my job away and
while I respected her for that I couldn't help but realise how
simple it would be if she did. Yes, I loved this job, it's been
my dream my whole life. She changed that though, now I
didn't want it if it meant I couldn't have her. My father
would clip my ears if he knew that, but if it was my mum or
his job, he would have picked her every time as well.

I got in my truck the drive to the racecourse would take just
over an hour and I had to be there early to help prepare. The
previous two days had gone well, and I hadn't seen Natalie

once but now on the last day, I feel my luck might run out. The journey was boring and left too much time for my mind to stray. Pulling into the car park couldn't have come quick enough, I needed to do something, anything, to stop my thoughts. Charlie was already there and handed me a coffee when I made it to our workspace. It wasn't much just an area where we could congregate and sort out what needed to be done. The coffee was at least good. He didn't say much outside of a good morning. I didn't know or care if Natalie had spoken to him about us. He hadn't yet commented so either she hadn't, or he was minding his own business.

The coffee was finished, and the hard work began, preparing the horses and the equipment for the day. Last-minute problems were not an option, so everything was checked and checked again.

There wasn't much to do once the races started so most of us took the opportunity to head out and find a spot to watch them. It was a gloriously sunny day as it always is at these things. It was as we were exiting the holding stalls that I saw her. She was with her family and him. Lord Penhall walked ahead chatting with a friend or acquaintance, her mother was slightly off to the side deep in conversation with Mr Layton. She walked alone looking like she would rather be anywhere else. Her miserable expression shocking against her attire. The flowers and formality sitting completely apart from her disposition. Lord Penhall greeted me, asking for a show of his horses to his friend whom he introduced as the Viscount of somewhere. I nodded leading them back into the building I had just left.

The Lord showed his friend between each stall, commenting on the work we had done. The other guys called out thanks as he praised them. Mr Layton, too, took an interest in the horses, giving a breakdown of his knowledge to Lady Francis. I stole looks at Natalie. She didn't return them keeping her expression flat and her eyeline steady on the wall. The ring was on her finger, I thought it would bother me. But seeing her so, unlike her was all I cared about.

They left to enjoy their day all of us wishing the other luck in today's races. She still hadn't looked at me.
We milled about for a while the guys all grabbing a drink and a sunny spot in view of the course. I stepped to the side pulling out my phone. Finding her name and tapping a quick message.

Where are you?

I didn't expect a response so when a moment later one pinged through it took me by surprise.

In the stands.

I turned running my eyes along the stand behind me, I couldn't make out much against the glare of the sun.

I can see you. A second message came through.

I smiled at it scanning the stands again.

Need a drink? I looked at some of the various stalls around me. Picking a random cocktail brand that had flags outside.
I hear 'Rosette' make a nice cocktail.

I might just have to try one then.

I read her reply making my way over to the tent and standing just outside of it. I didn't wait long before I saw her making her way through a throng of people. I pushed off from the tent walking towards the back buildings.

Everyone was either preparing for the race or readying to watch it, so when I picked a storage building and leaned against it, it was no surprise to not see anyone else. A few moments later she approached me. She looked nervous and still unsure.

"Hi." I tried a smile.

"Hey." She didn't look at me. I couldn't stand to see her down for one more minute. Grabbing the front of her dress I pulled her into me. Trying to kiss away all insecurity. "I'm sorry." She mumbled against my lips. I didn't need her apology. I just needed her. Pulling away I wiggled the door handle of the building. Finding it unlocked I opened it taking us both inside. It was lit enough from the one window, and I could see it was for spare seating and general event storage. Reaching up I flicked the lock on the top of the door. She eyed me, a small grin playing on her lips.

I took her hand, looking for a moment at the gaudy stone. I gently removed it placing it on the windowsill before turning back to her. She looked at me the nerves surging back for a moment. "When you're with me, I want you to be only mine." I murmured kissing her gently.

"Wherever I am, I'm yours." She deepened the kiss, pushing her tongue into mine. I grabbed her roughly, needy after the days we had spent apart. Lifting her dress, I let my hand trail into her underwear. Finding her soaking for me, I moaned as my fingers found their target. "Please, Luke." Her breathy begging at my ear. Tugging her pants down her legs, I spun her pressing myself to her back. I laid her down on a table.

I pulled down my trousers releasing myself, I palmed my hard length. "Do you want this, baby?" I asked for her permission as I teased her from behind.

"Yes, I want it." I pushed into her stopping only for a moment. I started moving, building my pace until I was crashing into her over and over again. Her cries of pleasure spurring me on. "Don't stop!" She cried out. *Wasn't planning on it princess.* Reaching around her never breaking stride I found her swollen mound again. Flicking my fingers over it helping her find her high. She came around me, squeezing me and shaking.

"Fuck." I cursed filling her and finally stilling. Leaning onto her back I pressed a line of kisses on her exposed skin before removing myself. I re-clothed myself before scanning the room. "Wait there." I commanded before going over to a cupboard. Opening it, it was full of table wear, I grabbed a pack of napkins before heading back to Natalie and cleaning up the mess I'd made.

Once done I helped her sort her dress out while she fixed her hair in her phone camera. "Can I see you tonight?" She asked still fixing her headband.

163

"Of course." She beamed at my response. "You should probably head back though before they wonder where you've gotten to."

She nodded though she didn't look like that's what she wanted at all. Pulling the lock-free she opened the door looking out first.

"Wait." I stopped her. Picking up the nearly forgotten ring from the windowsill, I handed it to her. "Can't have you getting into trouble." I knew what he was like, and I didn't want to give him any ammunition against her.

She kissed me lightly. "I'll see you later, enjoy the races." Then she was gone, taking the best part of my day with her.

18
Natalie

I stretched out on the sofa. This morning had been perfect. Luke had woken me with dozens of kisses all over my face. After spoiling me in the bedroom he made me a delicious breakfast. We then spent the rest of the morning cuddling on the sofa watching a film. It felt like such a normal couple thing to do.

Luke had just left to go to the manor. Some issue that they called him in to take care of. I now had the whole place to myself. I drifted upstairs to make the bed. Feeling on cloud nine and it was all thanks to him. Deciding then that I would show him how much it meant to me, starting with making him dinner tonight. And maybe serving myself as dessert. A dizzy excitement came over me and I rushed to get ready. I would need some ingredients but a quick trip to the shop would fix that.

Bounding back down the stairs, I grabbed my purse, coat and spare key before leaving. I hadn't stepped more than a few paces from the thresh hold when a voice called to me, instantly popping my happy balloon.

"I knew it." Peter moved from the fence post he was leaning against. "What are you doing here?"

"I could ask you the same thing." I raised an eyebrow.

"I was confirming a suspicion about my fiancé." He glowered at me, and I stared right back undeterred by the menacing look in his eyes. "Explain yourself."

"Explain what?" I replied showing how bored his company made me.

"Why you are in his house." He spat the words at me his voice a hiss of a whisper though there was no one around to hear us.

"No." I deadpanned.

He huffed running a hand through his hair and clenching the other. "Why are you here?" He steeled his back. "ANSWER ME!" He screamed at me. It sounded like a petulant child but there was something in his features, an anger I didn't want to test. I knew he wasn't above hurting me.

"Just visiting a friend." I wasn't about to tell him the truth but I'm also smart enough to know not to poke an angry bear.

"Lie." He spat.

"It's the truth."

"You often remove your engagement ring to visit 'a friend'." He stepped forward, and I stepped back.

"I often remove my engagement ring." I retorted like it was no big deal. "It didn't match my outfit."

"You fucking smart-ass." He laughed coldly taking a step towards me, my back now almost pressed against the cottage door. A thought flitted into my head, if I screamed now no one would hear me. I tried not to let that concern show on my face. "This is what's going to happen. You." He pointed at my chest. "Are going to stop whoring yourself out to that low life. You will break it off with him. You will start planning our wedding with enthusiasm. Then maybe I might decide to be lenient."

I didn't laugh, I might have normally, but I had never seen him look so venomous. "Lenient?" I questioned him not quite sure what cards he thought he held. He knew too damn well that I would never be enthusiastic to marry him or do what he tells me to.

He placed a hand next to my head and leaned in a smug grin on his face. "I'll be merciful to your little charity case." He ran his eyes down me. "I might see fit to be less rough with you too, at least our first time."

I wasn't sure if what he said was all true, but I felt bile rise, my throat constricting with fear. "I don't think either of my parents will let me marry you when you make those kinds of threats towards me, or their staff." I scratched my brain trying to think of anything to get him away from me. "In fact, I think I'll go talk to them now." To my surprise, he moved aside sweeping his arm in a wide gesture.

"Please do we can have an in-depth conversation about your activities. We can tell them together how I came here to confirm my suspicions. That you and he cooked up a plan to get you out of this marriage. How he sought to paint me as a bad guy, and how you opened your legs in thanks." He turned walking a few paces away. "Come on then." When he saw me hesitating, he spun back around. "That's right, best case scenario is you plant a seed of doubt in their heads. They might call off the wedding, but Mr Taylor will be fired. Dishonourably dismissed, no estate in the country would hire him. Worst case they believe me. I admirably forgive you; lover boy still gets fired, and we still get married. Most importantly though all ideas of leniency and mercy are gone." A deranged grin was now on his face. "I will take you, however I want. I will break you so easily." With every sentence, he stepped closer to me growing more and more demented. Putting his hand to my neck he moved my head and whispered in my ear. "I never lose." His tone was still sharp and deadly but with next to no volume, only intent and confidence. Tears ran down my cheeks and he placed a kiss beneath my ear. I wanted to throw up. Hit him. Scream. But I couldn't, I was frozen.
I would like to think that my parents would take my side, believe their child. But I wasn't so confident. I had done nothing but be difficult about this marriage. Coupled with Luke and Peter having priors, even I could see how it would look. Either way Luke and I lost. It was the main reason I had yet to tell them of what Peter had done to me. The

threats and bruises somehow didn't seem enough in my mind. They would think it exaggeration, my last-ditch attempt at breaking off this engagement.

I had never been so sure of someone's intentions as I was at that moment. I had underestimated my opponent. Thinking him a bully and a garden variety manipulator. Peter was much more than that, he was a spoilt resourceful conniving man. He had always got what he wanted, and he wasn't about to stop his winning streak. He pulled back straightening his suit jacket and brushing the sleeves down. His face had returned to the fake charm he was so learned at, he flashed me a toothy grin. "I shall see you later for dinner Natalie, I am going to assume my request will have been completed by that time. Enjoy the rest of your day." The venom in his tone having dissipated, there was no question in what he said. He knew I would do what he asked.

As soon as Peter left, I retreated inside. Shutting and locking the door just in case he decided to come back and make good on his threat. I slid down the cool wood trying to slow my erratic heartbeat. He was gone, I was safe inside Luke's house, but I still felt cornered. What do you do when fight isn't an option? You run.

By the time Luke stepped through the door, I had it all figured out. There was no scenario where this went well. None of the countless scenes I had played through in my head this past hour ended in anything other than complete heartbreak.

"Hey," I heard him call from the hallway. I nearly changed my mind. His voice, even now, calmed me. I would miss his voice. I had to do this. For both of us.

I had strategically sat myself in the armchair leaving him no choice but to sit apart from me. I needed to make this as easy as possible otherwise I would back out entirely. "Hi." I mumbled as he placed a small kiss on the top of my head. Pulling back, he took in my miserable expression.

"What's wrong? What's happened?"

I took a steadying drag of air. Just do it, Nat. Break his heart. "We need to talk." I motioned to the sofa. He sat on the footstool and placed a reassuring hand on my knee. "I think we should stop...seeing each other." I stared at my hands clasped in my lap.

"What?" I bought my eyes to his. I saw confusion and worry but not sadness. "Why?" He searched my eyes. "What happened?"

"Nothing, I just don't want to do this anymore."

He leaned back removing his hands. I realised that I should have savoured his touch, knowing I probably wouldn't feel it again.

"Really? Because I've been gone two hours and when I left that is not what I was getting from you."

"I was going to tell you this morning but then you got called out." I fumbled trying to make it sound pre-meditated.

"When? When we had sex, or perhaps during breakfast. When we sat right here watching TV together?" He had stood up and taken a few steps away from me.

"It's been on my mind for a few days."

He scoffed. "I don't believe you."

"I know I should have told y…"

"No, I really don't believe you, what aren't you telling me?"

I hadn't planned for him to just not believe me, and I needed him to know I was serious. He had to think this was my idea, otherwise, he would go after Peter, and this would end even messier. I stood also but kept my distance. "I am tired Luke. Tired of sneaking around. Tired of being at war with my parents. This was a stupid idea and yes for a while it was fun. But be honest did you see this going anywhere?" Lies all of it lies but I had to protect him and myself.

"So, you're what, giving up?" He ran a hand through his hair. "I only want you. I don't like sneaking around, but my solution would be to tell your parents. Not call it quits on the best thing that's happened to me." He tried to step

171

towards me but stopped when I receded back. "We can tell them today. We can do whatever you want."

"No!" I saw the defeat creeping into the edges of his face. I swallowed the lump of grief rising in my throat. "I don't want to." Do it, the rational voice in my head goaded. "You aren't listening to me. I don't want to be with you." I spelt it out slowly for him. "I don't love you." He looked like I had punched him in the gut.

"Nat, you don't…"

I cut him off. "I mean seriously I'm going to be the Lady of Brywood Manor someday, I can't be messing around with stable boys." Shaking my head, I picked up my bag and coat. Luke had panic and pain mixed on his handsome face. I wanted to kiss all the worry away, tell him I was sorry. Comfort him. But I couldn't so I said the only thing I could to drive the point home. "I am marrying Peter. I hope we can work together amicably in the future Mr Taylor." Then I left. Marching out of the house without looking back.

19
Natalie

Getting back to my room I didn't waste any time, I dialled Charlie's number, wedging the phone between my shoulder and ear. I waited for him to pick up as I went into my wardrobe. I had just grabbed two bags from a cupboard when he picked up, his cheerful tone playing in my ear.

"Hey Nat!"

"Charlie, I need your help."

My frantic tone must have scared him because his voice became concerned as he asked. "What's wrong?"

"I have to explain to your face, but I need you to meet me in the garage." I knew he would be suspicious, but he was the only one I knew would help me. "Don't tell anyone."

"I'll be there in ten." He hung up. I was going to miss him. I quickly shoved clothes into one bag, not caring what I picked up. I could buy new stuff later; I just needed a few days' worth. Taking the other bag around my room I grabbed my laptop and chargers for both it and my phone. Into the bathroom, I threw in makeup and a wash bag.

Picking up the engagement ring Peter had bestowed upon me I placed it open on my coffee table. I left no other note, knowing that my parents would get the message.

Hauling both now heavy bags onto my arms, I half jogged down to the garage. I didn't see a soul on my route, thankfully. Charlie was already there when I opened the adjoining door, he looked stressed. That amplified when he saw the bags in my hands.

"Natalie, what is going on?" He questioned me.

"I need to leave. Now." I pressed the button on my keys, unlocking my car.

"Why what's happened, have you killed someone?" He laughed slightly, trying to lighten the mood. When I didn't immediately respond he looked at me with wide eyes.

"Christ Charlie, no I haven't killed anyone." I ran a hand over my neck before meeting his eyes. "Remember when I told you I wouldn't get married to Mr Layton under any circumstance?" He just nodded in response. "Well, this is that circumstance, if I couldn't find a way out of it then I was going to leave." I took a deep breath. "I have no choice Charlie, it's not just about me anymore, I don't want to but I will protect myself and those I love."

"Luke." He spoke knowingly. I gaped at him; we had been more than careful. Both of us sure no one could know.

"How did you…"

"I've known for a while that there was something between you and when you two stopped spitting venom at each other I put two and two together." He looked sad for me now. "You can't tell him." I warned throwing both bags into the boot and chucking the keys at Charlie.

"Where are you going to go?" His question had me wondering whether I should tell him my whole plan.

"I'm not set on that yet, but I need you to drive me to a hotel for now. Then I need you to bring my car back and leave it here with the keys." I knew I was asking a lot, but I needed his help.

He breathed out a defeated sigh. "We best get moving then." He let himself into the car and I followed, quickly buckling. We sped out of the garage door and down the driveway. I took a last look in the rear-view at my home. I wasn't sure I would see it again.

We were silent for a while. I think Charlie was trying to wrap his head around the situation. Myself, I was trying not to panic and keep my head focused on what I had to do.

"I'll be getting rid of my phone." I told Charlie quietly his eyes snapping to me before returning to the road. "If it's OK I'll copy your number across and message you when I've done it." He nodded.

175

We pulled up to a quaint little hotel that couldn't be more than a few rooms. Cutting the engine off we sat in silence for a moment. "I'm sorry to have put you up to this Charlie." I mumbled looking at my hands.

He unbuckled himself before leaning over and squeezing me in a hug. "Don't apologise, I'm your friend and I want to help you, I just wish there was another way to do it."

"I know." I let a few tears stray down my cheek. "Me too."

Helping me lift the bags out of the boot he placed them on the hotel step before standing back and looking at me. Nothing but sadness in his eyes. "Make sure you message me regularly, tell me you're safe."

I nodded as he moved back round to the driver's side. "Keep being the bestest." I half waved at him. His smile didn't reach his eyes and then he was gone. I was completely alone now.

I sat in my hotel room trying to catch my bearings. I booked my flight as soon as I checked in and had arranged somewhere to stay, once I was back in New York. I had everything planned. Something that I couldn't plan for were my feelings. I wanted to turn back so badly. I wanted to go to Luke and apologise, beg him to forgive me. But I couldn't. Going back could only hurt him. I could tell my parents what Peter said. They would probably call off the

176

wedding, but I would have to explain Luke and me. He would lose everything, and we still wouldn't be able to be together. My mother would find another 'match' for me, and they would let me have even less freedom for fear of me running back to Luke. I had to stop spiralling.

Deciding to be proactive I left the hotel to go into the small town just down the road. Pulling a hat over my head, no one would be looking for me yet, but I didn't need a trail leading them to where I was. I found what I was looking for quite easily. Entering the small phone shop, I picked up the first one I saw and a pay-as-you-go SIM card. Taking both to the counter I paid in cash and left quickly. Of course, once I took my flight they would know I had left but I was hoping I would be anonymous until then.

Back in my room, I copied only two numbers to my new phone, Charlie and Maria, before taking my old SIM out and turning the device off. I texted Charlie first telling him I had a new phone and to not save my number. He replied saying he had gotten the car back in the garage without being seen and to stay safe. I would message Maria tomorrow with just a simple 'I'm safe.' they wouldn't be looking for me until then and I didn't want her to worry too much.

20
Luke

I confined myself to the house the rest of yesterday. Letting what Natalie had told me sink in. I couldn't believe it though. She had changed in a matter of hours. We had gone from a romantic morning to breaking up in the afternoon. Something had to have happened but whatever it was, was serious enough that she wouldn't tell me. I had dragged myself to work today hoping I might see her, hoping she might tell me. It had been less than 24 hours since she walked out of my house, but it felt like a lifetime. I loved her. No, I love her. And I didn't want to give up so easily.

I had been shuffling around the stables most of today keeping myself busy with odd tasks. Not wanting to shut myself up in the office where I might miss a chance encounter with her.

"Natalie?!"

I raised my head up from the straw I had been raking, hearing the calling from somewhere in the barn.

"NATALIE?!" Louder and more frantic came the second call.

I left my work, speed walking in the direction of the sound.
I nearly bumped square into Maria though she hardly
seemed to notice.

"Oh, Luke, my dear have you seen Natalie?" Her cheeks
were flushed, her eyes filled with worry and barely held
back tears.

"No why what's happened?" Concern creeping into my own
voice.

"Is Charlie around? Maybe she's on a lesson with him?"
She didn't answer my question instead asking more of her
own.

"No, he's got a day off today. Maria. Tell me what's
happened." I asked with more force this time grasping the
woman's shoulders to keep her in place.

"She's gone." She sputtered out. My hands falling from her
shoulders as she spoke.

"Gone?" I repeated in disbelief.

"She didn't show up for dinner last night nor breakfast or
lunch today. We thought she may have been out or at a
friend's, but her phone is off." She paused taking a big gulp
of air, the tears now flowing freely. "I checked her room
and it's been ransacked; half her things are gone and it's in
a right mess."

I pulled her close to me as she sobbed. "Shh, we will find her." I wasn't sure myself, but I had to hope we would. My concern grew to anger I knew whose fault this was. It was about time everyone else knew too. "Maria, I need to speak to Lord Penhall, where is he."

Wiping a few tears away she responded. "In his office, making some calls. The police." I didn't wait for her, heading off to the house. "Luke?!" She called after me, but I kept my pace. I didn't know if Natalie was safe and that was my main priority. I couldn't be sure Mr Layton hadn't done something, but I knew that either way he was to blame for this.

As I neared the manor I saw the offensive creature on the patio, he was smoking a cigarette looking exasperated. He saw me approaching and sneered at me from behind a billow of smoke. I snapped. Reaching him I grabbed his shirt collar, giving him just enough time to look offended before I punched the stupid look off his face. He stumbled back clutching his face, blood spilling from between his fingers. No sooner had he lowered his hand, his face contorted in a mess of blood and anger than I hit him again. Catching his cheek and hearing a satisfying thud as he fell to the floor. That felt good. He crawled back holding his hand up in a futile attempt to keep me at bay. Kneeling down I hit him again. And again. He really should have thanked Natalie for keeping me at bay, this was long overdue.

"LUKE!!!" Screaming had me stopping to look for the source. Maria had followed me and was stood on the patio looking white as a sheet. Her eyes flicked between myself and the bloodied Mr Layton. I shoved off of him and stalked into the kitchen satisfied to have that out of my system before Lord Penhall got his hands on him. I rinsed my knuckles under the tap, the blood wasn't my own and thankfully my skin hadn't split, though it was going to bruise like hell. Content that all traces of the beating were off, I made my way to Lord Penhall's office.

Approaching the door, I knocked and waited. Lord Penhall called from inside and I took one last confident breath before entering.

Byron was sitting in his place at the desk. He looked tired, his eyes dark and sunken into his face. Despite everything, I felt slightly pitiful of him. Lady Penhall was also in the room pacing in short lengths by the bookshelves. Her expression was one of desperation and worry. I had hoped to speak to the lord alone, knowing how Lady Francis could be, especially where Natalie was concerned. I would still say what I had to, reminding myself that this wasn't for me.

"Luke, this isn't a good time." Lord Penhall spoke his voice strained.

I sat anyway. "It's about Natalie."

"Do you know where she is?!" Lady Penhall's shrill voice came from her mid-stride.

I looked over to her hoping how sorry I was conveyed in my expression. "I don't, sorry."

She let out an exasperated sigh "Well, what is it then?" The Lord's voice had me returning focus to him. No backing out now.

"I'm in love with your daughter." I didn't stutter maintaining my stare on the Lord waiting for his reaction. He didn't look surprised.

"How dare you!?" Lady Penhall spat from where she still stood.

"How dare I what?" I once again looked over at the woman, her face now full of scorn. "How dare I love your daughter or how dare I tell you so?" When the only reply I got was her gaping at me I continued. "I love her because how could I not, I've loved her since we were children. And I'm telling you, only because I believe it will help her."

She scoffed at me. "Please you didn't love her. You had a silly crush that I told your father to put a stop to." Looking me over she added. "I see he failed."

I wasn't shocked that the order had come from her, though I was slightly disturbed that she would knowingly cause Natalie to be hurt. Given recent events maybe that shouldn't have shocked me either. "All that achieved was upsetting Natalie."

"Oh for goodness sake." She shook her head.

"Stop bickering." Lord Penhall ran a hand through his hair. "Is that all you came to say?"

"No, I came to tell you that you should call off her engagement."

"You would say that." Lady Penhall now stood by her husband.

"You should call it off because it's what she wants."

"She's just being petulant with this running away." she waved her hand like it was a game she was bored of. "She doesn't know what she wants. Mr Layton…"

"Mr Layton is an abusive prick." My words were vicious, but I didn't take them back. I ignored the outraged expression coming from his wife and spoke directly to the quieter spouse. "We never got to the ins and out of him trying to fire me, did we? He promised to assault your daughter at his earliest convenience. It didn't go down too well." I saw a switch go off in his features, once calm and measured now looked deadly. Imperceivable almost, except I had seen his calm features too often to not know the difference. "I know he has hurt her already; I'm assured he hasn't fully followed through on his vile threats. But I'm sure he would with half a chance."

"Lies, how could you possibly know that?"

I didn't even glance at her.

"Because I've seen the bruises and I held Natalie as she cried over them."

What I was saying dawned on them both, Byron Penhall looked slightly embarrassed, and Francis looked ready to kill me.

"You wretch…" She began but I didn't let her finish.

"I had to tell you I loved her so you would know I was telling the truth, up until the day she left I believed her to feel the same way for me." A small knot of sadness formed in my throat talking about her ending things. "She *was* happy, with me I mean, but her fear of him still drove her away. She did everything to protect me, work I'm undoing now by telling you all of this."

"If what you say is true." The Lady began.

"It is." I interjected.

"IF what you say is true," She repeated. "Then Natalie would have told us herself."

"Would she?" It was the Lord who spoke. He sounded disappointed but I got the feeling that had nothing to do with me and his daughter's affair.

184

"Of course she would have." Lady Francis argued, sounding more like she was trying to convince herself rather than her husband.

"At every opportunity for her to tell us, we shut her down. Drilling into her that it was her duty and tradition. I wouldn't be surprised to find out that she thought she couldn't tell us." The man turned to me now apology clear on his face. An emotion someone in his position didn't have to air often. "Luke, I need to know what he did."

I divulged everything I knew, every threat, every bruise, every comment. I spoke of how she had broken things off with me yesterday and my suspicions that Mr Layton had something to do with that also.

"I see. Then I think the next thing we need to do is have a discussion with Mr Layton and find out if he knows of Natalie's whereabouts." Byron's tone sounded business as usual, but I knew he believed me and there would be no saving Mr Layton now. He picked up the phone before speaking. "Maria, may you please ask Mr Layton to join me in my office." Placing it back down on his desk he clasped his hands together the knuckles turning white at the force he gripped with. Lady Penhall had been quiet for some time. Her aged but still beautiful features now sullen and filled with heartbreak and guilt. I felt bad for her but if only she had listened to her daughter.

A few moments later a light knock sounded on the door. Lord Penhall called entrance and a disgraced Peter entered. I didn't bother turning around, Lady Penhall's hand going to cover her mouth in shock. I smiled knowing my handiwork had left a dent in his pretty boy face. The Lord didn't comment though if I wasn't mistaken, I saw the corner of his mouth twitch with a hidden smile.

"What is the meaning of your condition?" Byron's frosty tone setting the mood.

I felt Mr Layton's glare on me from the adjacent seat. "Mr Taylor…" Byron stopped him raising his hand to halt any accusation.

"Mr Taylor has been in my office discussing the location of my daughter. You're not suggesting he was in two places at once." He paused looking at the damage done to his face. "Perhaps Maria has been working on her right hook." It was the first joke I think I had ever heard him crack and I bit my cheek to stop a laugh from escaping.

Peter looked utterly dumbfounded, he tried to sputter up a different excuse but couldn't find one. When he obviously couldn't think of anything to say he changed the subject. "Is there news on Miss Penhall?" I didn't miss the glance in my direction, was that fear in his eyes?

"We were hoping you could shed some light on that actually, Mr Layton." Lord Penhall accused.

"M...me?" Now he looked very nervous. "I have no idea where she is!" His voice was growing defensive.

"Please." I huffed, fed up with the constant manipulation from this arsehole.

He turned on me in an instant. "My Lord if you are looking for someone with information on Natalie's whereabouts, I suggest you aim your questions at the other seat." He smiled maliciously at me thinking he had me on the back foot. "Why don't you ask him about his recent activities."

"I don't need to." Byron sounding as fed up as me. "He has already told us. Everything."

The smile fell from Mr Layton's face, straightening his suit and sitting up trying to maintain some composure. "And were you just as shocked as I was to learn of this fornication?"

"Not really." The Lord deadpanned leading to more shock from all three other faces in the room. "Why did you assault Miss Penhall, Mr Layton?" Bryon's stare was deadly and non-yielding. When Peter didn't respond he pressed again. "Let me rephrase, you look confused. WHY DID YOU ASSAULT MY DAUGHTER?" His voice boomed out probably being heard throughout the manor. We all started a bit at the switch of volume. Peter looked like he might start crying at any moment, sick satisfaction rolled through me. This was almost better than breaking his nose.

"I. I. Well, I didn't think…" A mess of words tumbled from Peter's mouth, none of them confessions but all of them displaying his guilt.

"You would get caught? Anyone would notice?" Lord Penhall's voice was quieter though still loud enough to make an impact. "I'm taking your silence as guilt." I looked at the little worm next to me, his shoulders shaking slightly, Jesus, he might wet himself next. We all paused looking at Mr Layton, waiting for him to refute the charges. He did not. "Now do you have any idea where she is?" Shaking his head no longer meeting anyone's eye, Peter responded silently. "If it wasn't obvious your engagement is over. If I even catch a whiff of you anywhere near my family or anyone that I consider a friend, I will kill you. Do I make myself clear boy?!" Peter again nodded silently, accepting his defeat.

"My dear, would you show Mr Layton out and call for Maria?" Lord Penhall patted his wife's hand in a move and voice so gentle, jarring after the deadly display he had just shown. She nodded coming round from behind the desk. Mr Layton had stood to leave. Francis reached him and wordlessly slapped him around the face. His head whipped to the side. A sharp intake of breath came as he clutched his cheek. Lady Penhall shook her hand lightly before stepping to the door opening it and signalling for him to leave.

My eyebrows were still raised when I looked back at Lord Penhall who for the first time today, with all these confessions floating around, finally looked shocked. We shared a small half chuckle the older man composing himself as a soft knock came on the door. "Let's get Natalie home."

21

Natalie

I text Maria as I planned. Just a simple message telling her I was safe and to let my parents know I was safe. My phone started ringing almost immediately. Maria's name flashing on it. I ignored it letting it ring off on the bed next to me. As soon as it stopped it started again. She would stop eventually I told myself, trying not to make eye contact with the electronic. After she tried three times it stopped. I picked it up checking that she hadn't left a voicemail. It rang again in my hand, this time an unknown number showing. I bit my lip. It could be my parents. She undoubtedly told them. I let that one ring off too. Another number flashed on the screen. Then a third. And a fourth. I ignored all of them contemplating turning it off altogether.

It stopped for a while; I sat in silence as the minutes passed. I was partly scared they knew where I was and partly regretting not answering. Even if just to hear a friendly voice. My peace was broken by the now irritating ringtone again. I would have to change it after this. Rolling over from my pitying position in bed I picked it up. 'Charlie' illuminated on the screen. Sitting up straight I stared at it. He wouldn't phone unless it was important. What if something happened? In my contemplation, it rang off. I went to my contacts to message him when it started up again. This time I didn't hesitate, answering it on the first ring.

"Charlie?"

Relief flooded down the phone. "Hey Nat. His voice sounded relieved and guilty. Don't be mad."

I didn't have time to ask what he meant by that when another voice came down the line. "Natalie?" It was my father's. I didn't respond. "Please Natalie, come home."

"I can't." I replied quietly. "You know I can't."

"You don't have to marry him." I nearly dropped the phone.

"What?"

"Mr Layton, you don't have to marry him."

"What made you change your mind? How can I trust you?" I was sceptical, this could be a ploy to get me to go back, then they wouldn't let me leave. I doubt Charlie would have been involved in that though. And they couldn't honestly believe they could keep me trapped forever.

"We want to talk to you. We will explain everything but please come home." The Lord for perhaps the first time sounded vulnerable. I had not once heard my father beg for anything. But here he was on the other end of this phone begging me.

"I've booked a flight for tomorrow." Nothing from the other end. "If you're lying to me I will be on it." I paused a little longer. "I'll see you soon." Hanging up I scrunched the phone in my hand. I didn't fully trust this, but I had to know. If they meant it then I could go home. But why would they change their minds? Curiosity got the better of me and I packed quickly, calling a taxi as I did.

I took a deep breath before opening the front door. "Hello?" I called into the empty hall. I heard something clatter and footsteps sounding. Maria scurried into the foyer, wasting no time in hugging me all while telling me off.

"Why did you do that!? I was so worried!" She smacked my arm.

"Ow." I rubbed it where her hand had landed. "I'm sorry for making you worry." It was true, I didn't add that I had not yet cancelled my flight and fully intended on being on it if I caught even a whiff of a lie. "Where are they?"

"In Lord Penhall's office." She paused looking at me with concern. "Do you want me to come with you?"

I shook my head no.

Sitting in the chair in front of my father's desk I shuffled awkwardly. "Why didn't you tell us what Mr Layton had done." His voice cut through my nerves leaving confusion in their wake. How did they know about that?

"What do you mean?" I saved face, letting them show their hand first.

"We know...Everything." My mother's voice joined our conversation.

"Everything." I repeated.

"We know he hurt you and we know he made threats about you." My father looked sad and perhaps a little guilty.

"Oh. That." I fiddled with my fingers.

"Why didn't you tell us?"

"Would you have believed me?" I challenged. "Every time I tried you shot me down. Told me to behave."

They both looked a little guilty now. "Mr Layton is gone; we promise he will be nowhere near you ever again. We should have listened, but we never imagined everything that Luke said."

"What else did he say?" Shame flaring on my cheeks at exactly what Luke might have divulged to my parents.

"A lot." My mother's tone was clipped.

"Are you angry with me?"

"No." Came my father's response taking me a little by surprise. "We are just glad you're safe. Natalie, I am so sorry I didn't listen." His apology healed a small part of me. Tears formed but I pushed them down.

"And what of Luke is he in trouble?" I looked between them.

"Well, we haven't…" My mother spoke first, the Lord interrupting whatever she was going to say.

"No." my father looked at my mother. "He isn't in trouble."

I nodded my head relief washing through me. "So, what happens now?" They had explained that I didn't have to marry Mr Layton, but I doubt they will let me gallivant around with a grounds manager.

"You still need to marry." My mother's tone was gentler than usual. Probably scared I'll run away again. "Eventually." She sighed resolution lacing the sound. "Maybe we can pick someone together, so this sort of thing doesn't happen again." This was her way of admitting she was wrong, and for her, the nearest to a sorry I was going to get.

My father interjected. "Did you want to marry Luke?"

Both Lady Francis and I probably wore similar faces of astonishment.

"I, uh, well." I stumbled over the words.

"Don't be ridiculous!" The lady beside the lord finally protested. "She can't marry a stable boy!" she whisper hissed.

"OK." I held my hands up stopping everyone. "First off, he is a grounds manager, not a stable boy. Father is always talking about the needs of the manor and the responsibilities it entails. Luke knows more about that than all of us except Father. So, in that respect, the very reason you say I can't, makes him a perfect choice." I looked at my father. "I don't know. If I want to marry him. It's not something I have been able to think about, being that I was supposedly engaged until today." Sorrow weighed in my chest as I spoke. "We aren't together any more regardless. I doubt he will speak to me after what I said and leaving as I did."

"Maybe." A small smile played on the corner of my father's mouth. Tapping a pen idly against his desk. "I have a proposition for you Natalie." I raised my brows in response. "You can explore your options with Luke or someone else if that is what you desire. And we will revisit the idea of a marriage in a couple of years."

I could have burst with happiness. I was free. A huge smile plastered itself to my cheeks. "Really?"

"You want me to change my mind?" He jested.

I shook my head. "No no no!"

My mother opened her mouth to protest, shutting it again. Sighing she rolled her eyes. "Fine. But you aren't off the hook, you must marry one day. And we must approve of your choice."

My turn to roll my eyes.

I nodded before getting up from my chair and going around the desk. First, I hugged my mother. She was taken aback stiffly hugging me in return. Next, I threw my arms around my father who remained seated. He patted my hands crossed over his chest. "Thank you," I whispered in his ear planting a kiss on his cheek.

"May I go?" I asked.

A nod released me, and I almost sprinted from the room. Heading for my next destination.

Charlie was outside pacing on the patio, his head snapping up when I walked through the French doors. "I am so sorry! I know you didn't want me to tell anyone, but they said you wouldn't have to marry, and they just wanted you home safe. Maria was crying!" He held my hands guilt all over his face.

"Charlie. Charlie. CHARLIE!" I stopped his apologies. "It's fine."

Standing back, he looked at me warily. "It is?"

"Of course. You're a good friend and I asked too much of you. You did the right thing." He hugged me until I thought my shoulder would pop out.

Sighing with relief. "So, I'm still the bestest, that's good."

I laughed hitting his back. "Get off me!" He did as I asked releasing me from his death grip. "Where is he?" I asked nervously.

Nodding his head down the garden. "Stables." Seeing me hesitate he slung an arm over my shoulder. "I'm going that way. Walk with me," He spoke steering me down the path. We didn't talk but I was glad for the company.

Releasing me by the stables he pointed inside. "He should still be in the office. Call me if you need me." Then he was gone, and it was just me and my nerves.

After deliberating on just running back to the house I knocked on the door.

"Come in." His voice muffled from behind the wood, called me into the room. I walked in carefully, not entirely sure on the reaction I would get. He stood immediately from his desk, the chair scraping back and nearly toppling. "Nat."

197

"Hi." It was all I could think to say, this was more awkward than I wanted but not any less than I deserved. I walked a little further into the room closing the door. "I wanted to come and apologise."

He shook his head. "You don't have to…"

"No, I do." Clasping one hand in the other I looked at him. He didn't seem angry or upset any more. "I need to say I'm sorry for running off. And I'm sorry for what I said. And I am very sorry that you were the one to tell my parents what you did. That should have been me."

"Actually, I think me telling them is what made them believe it." He smiled a little.

"You're probably right they would have assumed it was a line to get me out of marrying… regardless I am sorry it can't have been easy."

"You should have seen your mum's face when I told them. Especially certain details." His smile turned mischievous.

I squeezed my eyes shut cringing at the thought. "Oh god, that must have been a picture." I laughed a little shaking my head. "I did ask if you were in trouble, they said you weren't. So, your position is safe."

He nodded slightly looking at the desk before meeting my eye. "I don't care. They could have told me I would never work again, and I still would have said what I said Natalie."

"But you love this job," I argued back, knowing he was being polite.

"Jesus woman. Sure I do. But I love you more."

"What?"

He closed the gap taking my hands and turning them over in his. "Did you mean what you said to me in my house? That you don't love me. That it was all just a bit of messing around?"

"No, I didn't mean any of it. I just needed to push you away."

"Good, that's good."

I looked at his face, as gorgeous as the first day I stepped into this office. It seemed so long ago. "Can we start again?" He looked at me a little puzzled. I stepped back holding my hand out. "Hi, I'm Miss Penhall, please call me Natalie." I smiled at him.

He took my hand in his, instead of shaking it pulling me into his chest. "Nice to meet you Natalie, but can we skip a few steps?" He pressed his lips to mine. Holding me, he kissed me like it was the first time

About the Author

Alexandra Kate is an aspiring author from the English Riviera. She lives there with her husband, their naughty beagle and a very spoilt ginger tom cat. Being a hopeless romantic at heart her favourite topic of writing consists of the kind of love that can be so rare but so deserved. In her spare time, she likes to kayak and swim in the sea, when the weather is sunny enough. She does still live in England. Spending the winter and more often than not rainy times, reading, knitting and drinking far too much coffee.

Printed in Great Britain
by Amazon

28857213R00116